Dear Reader,

Home, family, community and love. These are the values we cherish most in our lives–the ideals that ground us, comfort us, move us. They certainly provide the perfect inspiration around which to build a romance collection that will touch the heart.

And so we are thrilled to offer you the Harlequin Heartwarming series. Each of these special stories is a wholesome, heartfelt romance imbued with the traditional values so important to you. They are books you can share proudly with friends and family. And the authors featured in this collection are some of the most talented storytellers writing today, including favorites such as Roz Denny Fox, Margaret Daley and Mary Anne Wilson. We've selected these stories especially for you based on their overriding qualities of emotion and tenderness, and they center around your favorite themes–children, weddings, second chances, the reunion of families, the quest to find a true home and, of course, sweet romance.

So curl up in your favorite chair, relax and prepare for a heartwarming reading experience!

Sincerely,

The Editors

MARGOT EARLY

has written stories since she was twelve years old. She has sold over three million books with Harlequin Books; her work has been translated into twelve languages and sold in dozens of countries. Ms. Early lives high in Colorado's San Juan Mountains with two German shepherds. She has studied herbalism and martial arts, and she enjoys the outdoors, spinning dog hair and dancing with Caldera, a tribal belly-dance troupe. You can find her on Facebook.

HARLEQUIN HEARTWARMING

Margot Early

A Little Learning

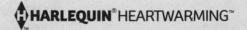
HARLEQUIN® HEARTWARMING™

Recycling programs
for this product may
not exist in your area.

ISBN-13: 978-0-373-36611-8

A LITTLE LEARNING

Copyright © 2013 by Margot Early

Originally published as GOOD WITH CHILDREN
Copyright © 2007 by Margot Early

Printed in U.S.A.

H HARLEQUIN®
™ www.Harlequin.com

A Little Learning

For Chris

"The story of one's life as it is written
into the body can be retold and understood
in the intense moment of dancing."
—*Grandmother's Secrets* by Rosina-Fawzia Al-Rawi,
translated by Monique Arav

CHAPTER ONE

Sultan, Colorado
January

RORY GORENZI WAS on time for the 10:00 a.m. meeting with her father. She was usually punctual and she'd never lost a job because of absenteeism or tardiness. She'd lost none of her previous jobs because of incompetence, either. Instead, she had lost them for speaking before thinking—or, rather, for speaking her mind as her thoughts occurred.

It was imperative that she keep her mouth shut now. She wouldn't say *anything* unless her father required her to speak.

But she *would* focus on the conversation at hand, rather than dwelling on her recent loss or on the other minor problem in her personal life. The problem wasn't really *her* problem: a disagreement among her fire-dancing/belly-dancing troupe regarding a living creature in the household they shared. A living creature that had long since ceased to be useful to their troupe, a living creature that no zoo or reptile rescue facility had so far agreed to adopt.

It was a bad situation, but Rory couldn't think about it now.

Nor could she think about her beloved pet, Gandalf, now, or she would break down in tears. The vet had put down the old dog after a long illness only the day before. Now, he was out of pain, at last, and she mustn't cry about that.

In his office at the Sultan Mountain School, Kurt Gorenzi sat behind a scarred walnut desk, a remnant of Sultan's earlier mining days. His hair was thick, gray-flecked, wavy, a little long. Rory's curls, sun-lightened brown and reaching to her waist, had come from him, from her father. As had her nose—straight, lightly dusted with freckles. And her brown eyes.

It was unlikely that her personality had been influenced by him, however, since she'd had little contact with him over the years, despite having grown up in the town of three hundred where he lived.

Kurt Gorenzi wore a plaid flannel shirt, Carhartts and Sorels. The driving force behind Sultan's recently reborn economy looked like the unapproachable mountain man he was. He stood when she entered, considered her formally, did not invite her to sit—and did the talking. "You'll be forming the program for Seamus Lee's family," he said. "I've given them the Empire Street house, and they're bringing a dog."

A dog.

Gandalf had been fourteen, old for a German shepherd.

She blinked away the thought of Seamus Lee's dog. Rory was unlikely to have another of her own—not now, in any case. She lived with the two other members of Caldera, one of whom was allergic to both dogs and cats and had put up with Gandalf only because Rory had refused to live there without him.

"Seamus Lee is a cartoonist and animator," Kurt continued. "He employs five people full-time in Telluride and is considering moving his business and family to Sultan. He has four children."

Rory understood the importance of all this. Four children was four children's worth of funding for the public school. Five full-time employees meant population and economic growth.

"He and I have known each other for—well—a while. We were skiing buddies years back, during a winter I spent in Telluride. He wants to get his kids out of there because he thinks they're being corrupted by the..." He chose his words carefully. "Atmosphere of affluence."

She pressed her lips tightly together, finishing his sentence in her mind. *The atmosphere of affluence that you hope to bring to Sultan.* Her self-restraint made her proud.

"But none of that is relevant. In fact, the family's enrollment at the school wasn't his idea. He received an anonymous gift package and he's agreed to take it.

"They're signed up for a three-month program, and I need you to plan activities that will give the kids each three months' worth of school credit. Except for the youngest, who's just four."

"Four?" echoed Rory. The Sultan Mountain School provided an outdoor education, as well as academics, for children as young as kindergarten age and up to grade 12, and, in certain cases, even offered university credit. The academic work was tailored to complement outdoor programs and provide school credit for the periods enrolled children would be absent from their regular schools. The longest SMS program lasted three months.

"In this packet—" Kurt handed her a thick ten-by-thirteen envelope "—you'll find background to fill you in on the Lees' skills and interests."

"Is the dad supposed to get school credit, too?" That didn't sound the way she had intended it to sound. "I just mean," she said, "what is he looking for?"

"Exactly what the Sultan Mountain School offers. Backcountry experience, tutorials in free-heel skiing and ice-climbing, natural history, mountain science..."

And more. The Sultan Mountain School was dedicated to "increasing appreciation for the mountain environment through education and experience."

Of course, SMS wasn't the only local enterprise that bore Kurt Gorenzi's fingerprints. He was a town council member and he'd even helped create the Sultan Childhood Learning Center—ironic, thought Rory, considering how much he'd had to do with his *own* child's early life. He'd led the push for the Sultan Recreation Center and had brought a chairlift to Silver Slope, the town's small family ski area. He'd helped restore a historical mining tramway up into Eureka Gulch for the use of sightseers and had promoted kayaking and river rafting on the Sultana River. He'd done everything he could to keep the town of Sultan, elevation 9,632 feet, from dying. But this was the first time he'd made Rory part of one of his projects.

He hadn't sought her out. She'd applied for the job of instructor and assistant director of the Sultan Mountain School. Her father had interviewed her, had made no comment regarding her extensive and varied work history and then he'd hired her. It was the first time in her life she'd ever asked him for anything. She couldn't remember her mother, who'd died when she was small; she'd been raised by her mother's mother. Her father had simply cut himself out of her life, although she knew he'd given Gran money every month to support them both financially.

And now, as during her interview, she was grateful to him for not mentioning the reason

she'd been fired by the State of Colorado—
which the entire town knew. She'd been an
avalanche researcher with the misfortune to
be in the field when a United States senator from Colorado accompanied a Realtor
and a land developer into a backcountry
area just outside Sultan. The group of visitors had stopped to ask about her work and
she'd demonstrated the volatility of current
avalanche conditions, using a snow pit she'd
just dug. After they told her their destination,
listened to her strenuous advice to avoid the
area because of *extreme* avalanche danger
and started forward anyway, she'd said, *Are
you on crack?* Which was probably not the
most tactful way to comment on their fool-
hardy behavior.

The senator, to his credit, had tried to prevent her from being fired—he was a politi-
cian after all and no doubt wanted her vote.
But the Realtor also had friends in high
places, and he had been massively annoyed.

Her previous job had been with the local
towing company. Speaking too frankly to
customers who told her how to use equipment they'd never been trained to use had
cost her that job. Well, actually, it was one

snowy night when she'd finally said, *Fine.
I've got other calls. Dig it out yourself.*

She had taught skiing at Silver Slope until
she'd told one parent that he was spoiling his
daughter and turning her into a brat.

She'd taught avalanche-awareness classes
over the mountains in Telluride until a wolf
dog she was watching for a boyfriend de-
stroyed four beacons and two shovels she'd
left in her car. He'd also consumed the passenger seat, but since the avalanche school
didn't own that, it hadn't figured in the com-
plaint. Rory'd replaced the equipment, which
had left her in debt, but it hadn't mattered.

This time, however, nothing was going
to go wrong. She reached for the packet.
"Sounds good. When will they be here?"

His lips smiled slightly. "Today."

Rory nodded. "I'll get right on this, then.
Thank you." She didn't say for what, because
her gratitude took in so many things. *Thank
you for giving me a chance. Thank you for
believing in me.*

Thank you for noticing me.

She was at the door when her father spoke.
"Where is the snake?"

Rory bit her lip. Of course her father knew

about Lola; everyone in Sultan knew. He probably *didn't* know Rory had just put down Gandalf. "At the house," she said. "She's... contained."

"Maybe," her father suggested, "you three should simply move her home outside."

"Yes," was all Rory said. Let Lola freeze? At the moment, and despite Rory's recent loss, the suggestion was not entirely unappealing. Besides, snakes were different from dogs, and Rory could not believe that Lola had any feelings whatsoever for her human family. Finally, she said simply, "She's not my snake."

Just a member of her household.

SEAMUS LEE HAD a career, money, four children and a recent ex-girlfriend who had left him burdened with a wealth of accusations he was having trouble clearing from his mind.

Every girlfriend you've had since Janine died has just been a glorified nanny.

Unfair. He'd *always* employed an *au pair,* in addition to Fiona Murray, who was essential to his household, far more than just a nanny or housekeeper.

And it's not as though you're any kind of a

father. They might as well be orphans, Elizabeth, his ex, had continued.

He should never have gotten involved with one of his artists. Yes, she was a freelancer; and yes, she had income independent from what he provided. In fact, she was loaded and she worked because she wanted to, not because she had to. He'd wondered if *she* was behind the anonymous gift he'd received of a deluxe term at the Sultan Mountain School. Elizabeth had certainly approved.

The drive to Sultan will probably be the most time you've spent with them since their mother died, she'd said.

AND THAT, UNFORTUNATELY, was too close to true. So he'd accepted the gift without knowing who was behind it. He would spend this time with his children.

He would manage *without* Fiona.

Well, not the entire time. His seventy-three-year-old household manager would be joining them after a month of sea kayaking in Mexico with her son and his wife.

So *alone* he was taking the children out of school in Telluride, Colorado, where his own business—the empire of Ki-Rin, the *manga* and anime character, half-boy, half-dragon—thrived, and over two mountain passes to Sultan to spend three months at the Sultan Mountain School. There, the children would receive school credit while improving their skills as snowboarders, skiers and mountaineers *and* learning mountain science. The characteristics of aspens and ponderosa pines, the mechanics of avalanches, the rules of water. Four-year-old Belle would learn to ski. And Seamus would demonstrate that "we never stop learning," by completing the three-month course alongside them.

He would also prove that he was not the stranger to his own children that his ex-girlfriend had seemed to think he was. At least she hadn't also become an ex-employee.

I have no problem with your art, she'd said. *It's very accessible. But you're not.*

Not emotionally accessible?

Well, there might be reasons.

As there was also a reason—a *good* reason—why he approached any time alone with his children with extreme caution. There was part of his emotional makeup that he definitely wanted to keep inaccessible to them, for the sake of the family's survival.

He drove a new Toyota SUV hybrid, the latest in nanny cars. It was his first trip anywhere in the vehicle, which had been the previous *au pair*'s car while she lived with them.

Now, fourteen-year-old Lauren had claimed the front passenger seat. In the back, twelve-year-old Beau and seven-year-old Caleb took the window seats while Belle, in her special car seat, endured the position of the youngest—the middle of the backseat, with her stuffed animal, a mouse, in her lap. Behind them, in a metal dog crate, rode the family's new pet, Seuss, a twelve-week-old German shepherd.

The drive to Sultan took seventy-four minutes. It felt like seventy-four days, however, with Belle asking far too often when Fiona would be back.

"I hate this town," Lauren announced, glowering as they passed the first junk store on the edge of town—The Sultan Flea Market. "The people are, like, backward."

Another good reason to spend some time out of Telluride, Seamus thought. Sure, Telluride was "a great place to raise kids," with world-class skiing, good schools, culture, of a sort, and natural beauty. But he'd noticed a tendency in his children to see themselves as intellectually brilliant and world-class athletes. Seamus, born and raised in the Silicon Valley in California, surrounded by exceptional brains, the brother of a cyclist who'd finished near the top in the Tour de France, knew his children to be simply "above average." And more than a bit snotty.

They *were* beautiful children. Beau was the only one of the four without a horde of friends. He wore white T-shirts on which he wrote, in magic marker, obscure quotations from obscure texts, sometimes in dead languages. Beau actually *might* be brilliant, a thought that terrified Seamus. Already, he was studying trigonometry and his first love was chess. He had little interest in snowboarding, skateboarding or skiing, and spent too much time indoors playing video games on his computer. Now, Lauren gazed through the windshield with visible dissatisfaction. She'd been chosen homecoming princess of the freshman class that fall. She was so popular and had so many friends that she hadn't wanted to leave—not even for three months. Caleb was a soccer star and an easy child. And Belle…

Elizabeth's words pounded at him again. He just didn't know Belle.

Seamus had memorized directions to the historic hotel that was the home base for the Sultan Mountain School. He would meet his old friend Kurt there and pick up the keys to the house.

The hotel was three storeys high, with its historic name, the Hotel Ambassador, painted on the brick facade. A shingle hanging over the street, a block from Main Street, read, SULTAN MOUNTAIN SCHOOL. Seamus parked.

Beau shoved open his door. "I'm going to get Seuss out, okay?"

"Put his leash on him," Seamus ordered. German shepherds were supposed to be smart, but he hadn't seen many signs of intelligence in Seuss so far. He did have a startling baritone bark—strange coming from a puppy.

As Lauren climbed out and stalked to the rear of the vehicle, no doubt intending to criticize her brother's behavior with the dog, Seamus headed for a wood-and-glass door beneath the shingle. It opened as he reached it and a young woman came out, almost colliding with him. She had long, thick hair, curly and tied back in a loose ponytail. Her eyes were brown, her nose straight and lightly sprinkled with freckles. The eyes widened slightly at the sight of him and his vehicle. "You're… You're Mr. Lee," she exclaimed, and shifted a manila envelope, book and a huge, lumpy package, then held out her hand. "You are, aren't you? I'm Rory Gorenzi."

"Any relation to Kurt?"

"Ah, yes. Yes. I'm his daughter, actually." As if the fact surprised even her. "And you *are* Seamus Lee?" She sought confirmation again.

"Yes." Kurt's daughter was beautiful. He'd heard about her from Kurt: she'd been raised by her grandmother, Seamus was fairly certain, and she wasn't as successful as Kurt wished, though Seamus didn't know the details. Seamus hadn't paid much attention to Kurt's conversation on the matter—he'd been too worried that his own children might not turn out all right because they, like Rory Gorenzi, had no mother.

And if Elizabeth was right, an inaccessible father.

It was over three years since Janine's death.

There had seemed to be no time for his own mourning, not to mention his accompanying feelings, with his youngest child just one and not even weaned when everything changed. With the whole story unfolding around him.

How his wife had come to die that way. And his inner conviction that her death had been her own fault. Her most aggravating traits had led to her dying, and he still couldn't forgive her—and couldn't speak to his children because he was afraid he'd tell them how angry he was at their mother for being so fatally single-minded.

Immediately after Janine's death, the succession of *au pairs* had begun.

He dragged himself away from his grim thoughts.

Rory Gorenzi wore a black snowboarding jacket, black snow pants, Sorel-style boots and mittens. Both jacket and pants were patched with duct tape, and the boots had seen more than a few seasons. "Look," she said, "I've got the key to your place, and I'll take you over there. I just need to quickly run down there…" She indicated an area across the street and half a block up, "and drop off this stuff."

"Can I help you?" He reached out, offering to relieve her of her package, which seemed not only oddly shaped but heavy.

She sidestepped him. "Oh, I'll get it. It's, um, pet food. Just let me… Just—I'll be right back." She turned away and tripped over a crack on the sidewalk, and the parcel, envelope and book all flew out of her arms and landed in front of her, the brown paper ripping to reveal what were unmistakably dead rabbits—frozen.

Seamus ran his tongue around the inside of his cheek and bent to pick up the book and envelope while she reached for the rabbits.

"My roommate bought these in Montrose," she explained. "Usually we have them shipped, but we ran out and had to get some while we're waiting for our next order to arrive. I realize it looks odd. They're for a snake. It's not mine."

The snake must be large, Seamus thought, to eat full-grown rabbits.

He glanced back toward a sound behind him, to find his two oldest children and Seuss, the puppy, all breathing steam in the frigid air and gazing at the scene before them with a mixture of disbelief and puzzlement.

Seuss had one ear up and one ear down, and Rory Gorenzi suddenly swallowed hard and looked away. Seamus had the strangest feeling that she was about to cry.

She said, shakily, "My dog was just put down yesterday."

"I'm sorry," Seamus responded politely. Though he couldn't really imagine crying over a dog. He'd never had one until now, and he'd only agreed to the puppy in order to demonstrate, at least to himself, that he *did* have a relationship with his kids.

Rory seemed to make up her mind about something. She crouched down and looked at the puppy, who immediately came toward her and sat down, leaning against her legs as if finally he'd found security. "You're a handsome guy," she said.

Eyeing the frozen rabbits with disgust, Lauren looked as though all her suspicions about the residents of Sultan had been confirmed. "What are those for?"

"My roommate has a…well, a Burmese python. She's sort of all of ours, but…"

"Can we see it?" asked Beau, unusually engaged. "Can we watch it eat?"

"Eating's maybe not the best time to see

her," Rory said apologetically. "She's a bit unpredictable then."

"How big *is* this creature?" asked Seamus, inexplicably fascinated by Kurt Gorenzi's daughter.

"Well, almost thirteen feet. And she has a nice disposition. It's just that, well, the disposition doesn't exactly matter with a snake that size. If you see what I mean. Because she weighs about sixty pounds, we follow a protocol when we clean the vivarium or feed her. There always have to be two of us, and preferably three on hand. Actually, we're trying to find a zoo or reptile rescue place to accept her, because she's really gotten too big for us to care for. That's probably much more than you wanted to know about Lola."

Lauren picked up Seuss and gazed at Rory as if *she* were a python who might suddenly decide to eat the puppy.

Seamus wondered just what Rory's "roommate" was like. A boyfriend with a Harley and a love of gigantic pythons?

She wrested the book and envelope away from him and said, "I'll just go to my house, and then I'll be right back. After that, I'll take you to the place where you'll be staying—

it's right around the corner from where I live. Across the alley, so it's on the next street, but…I'll be back."

Rory hurried away, stepping carefully over the ice on Solomon Street and imagining Seamus Lee and his two children watching her.

He was handsome. She supposed she should have expected he would be one of those Telluride types, probably a regular speaker at the film festival and probably with his own private jet tucked into a hangar at the airport. If he wasn't rich, he looked like he should be. Those new hybrid SUVs weren't cheap, in any case.

His hair was a bit long and so dark brown it was almost black; his features angular. He was six feet, definitely, and dressed in Gore-Tex and Carhartts. Very Telluride. Very Colorado. Very ski resort. His eyes were green, a true green and not remotely hazel. Probably around forty, she thought. Probably divorced, she also thought. She should know, but she hadn't even had a chance to look at the packet her father had given her. She'd just had time to get the rabbits out of the school freezer, where Desert had left them in a rush the previous afternoon on her way to an appointment. Desert, the founder of Caldera, their dance troupe—was a massage therapist at the local hot springs; her current boyfriend worked at the mountain school. Lola belonged to Desert, and Rory could not believe that Desert had just casually left the rabbits in the freezer here. *Is she trying to ruin my working relationship with my father before it even begins?*

That wasn't Desert's style, though. Desert simply felt that, well, people should be able to cope with just about anything. She thought rabbits in the freezer were not a big deal, and they were no problem for Rory; but other people might not feel that way. Desert also thought it shouldn't have been a problem for the State of Colorado, if Rory was less than polite when speaking to a U.S. senator.

Her roommates were home.

In fact, they were treating the frigid day as good weather, and spinning poi—firelit balls attached to cables—out in their backyard. Rory wished she could practice with them, as she'd planned to do, but Seamus Lee and his family had arrived sooner than expected. She hadn't even had time to figure out their course work. Samantha, whose white-blond hair was pulled into a knot at the back of her head and covered with a tight-fitting ski hat, was the spotter, standing by with a fire blanket, just in case. Without taking her eyes from Desert, Samantha edged to the fence to greet Rory.

Desert, whose head was entirely shaven beneath *her* ski hat, ignored the approach of her roommate and continued spinning the burning balls. Total concentration was required, and still poi spinners got burned. Samantha asked, "Did you bring the rabbits?"

"Yes," Rory said, with resignation, letting herself in the back gate. She and Samantha were of one mind about Lola—the python had to go. Samantha now refused to have anything to do with the snake beyond assisting—from a safe distance—at feeding time. She'd been bitten the previous summer and she was convinced the snake would have killed her—by constriction—if both Desert and Rory hadn't been there to pull it off. As it was, she'd needed sixteen stitches to close the bite.

Rory agreed that the snake might have killed Samantha. In fact, Lola had frightened Rory more thoroughly than anything else ever had in her entire life. And Rory was *not* afraid of snakes.

She wanted to plead with Desert not to do anything that might jeopardize her job. But Desert wouldn't welcome an interruption to her practice. And on second thought, Rory didn't think she was up to coping with Desert at the moment.

Desert, christened Naomi Katz, had come to Colorado at the age of eighteen. She'd immediately rechristened herself and had begun living off a trust fund provided by her grandfather, a diamond broker, and also by her mother's family. Rich and beautiful, she'd trained in Boulder as a massage therapist and as a fire dancer, had moved to Sultan and bought the two-storey Victorian where she, Rory and Samantha now lived. Its exterior was painted pink.

Sometimes, Rory and Samantha asked themselves why they put up with Desert.

But they loved her. And pitied her. And wanted to help her somehow; help her to not make life hard for herself. Desert's boyfriend was a recent acquisition—they'd been together nine weeks. Rory and Samantha were holding their breaths, dreading the ending.

Dreading it for themselves as well as for Desert, who was sensitive and, well, troubled.

Rory said to Samantha, "Can you take these? I've got to go show some clients to the Empire Street house."

"Sure." Samantha took the rabbits, clutching the bundle against her with one arm. "Go."

RORY GORENZI WAS ATTRACTIVE, but Seamus had come from Telluride, where beautiful was the norm. He didn't want another girlfriend; he only wanted to sort through the things his ex-girlfriend had said. He wanted to attend to the flaws she'd pointed out. And they were flaws. He didn't want to marry again—his experiences with other women reminded him not that Janine had been the perfect wife and mother, but that she hadn't been. No, that wasn't fair. She'd been the mother of their kids and, so, the perfect mother for them.

But she'd always needed to prove something. *He'd* known she was sensitive beneath her sometimes-abrasive exterior. One of his male employees had once said to Janine, "You have more testosterone than I do."

She'd said, "Thank you!" and had clearly been pleased by the compliment.

She'd been an athlete, but that wasn't the only thing that had made her challenging. It was the way she'd presented herself. Her certainty that *her* way was right. She'd been insecure and determined to hide the fact, and in their twelve years of marriage she'd never revealed the source of that insecurity or the reason for it.

She'd been smart—a legal-aid lawyer employed by the Women's Resource Center, defending the battered and the terrified. And she'd never struck him as particularly maternal, although she'd nursed each child for at least nine months.

Janine had been difficult, and since her death Seamus had vacillated between the notion that no relationship could be as trying as his marriage had been and the idea that no woman would be as good for his children as Janine had been. And how good was that, really?

Better than you, Seamus.

But that hadn't been so true, back when his wife was alive. He'd spent time with his kids, talked with them and listened to them.

Janine had listened, too—long enough to get the gist of situations. Then, she'd pronounced judgment. *You're not going to take that from anyone,* she would order the seven-year-old who'd just had his lunch money stolen.

Lauren seemed determined to remember her as a sort of warrior mother, an Amazon who had demanded warrior-like behavior from her children, as well. Even these days, Seamus occasionally heard his oldest say, "Mom wouldn't have stood for that," or "Mom wouldn't have put up with that."

But actually, she might have. To be as much bite as bark required a certain resolve that she'd lacked. Janine had been a great skier, a hard-riding cyclist, a distance runner, a strong ice-climber and, above all, a fantastic talker. She had talked big. It was the one quality that had come to define her and that Seamus had eventually found most annoying.

Seamus went inside the Sultan Mountain School to see if Kurt was around. Lauren accompanied him, leaving Beau, Caleb and Belle outside with Seuss.

As they stepped into the lobby of the Victorian building, Seamus spotted Kurt, talking to two men in mountaineering clothes and showing them something on a topographical map on one wall. Seamus saw that the map was composed of many geological survey maps joined together.

"You don't want to go that way," Kurt was saying. "Too much avalanche danger. I'd recommend taking the V-Dot Road...."

Lauren said, "There's not going to be anything to *do* here."

"You're going to have plenty to do."

"I don't want to spend three months snowshoeing."

"Somehow, I don't think that's what Ms. Gorenzi has in store for you."

"Is she going to be our teacher?" Lauren seemed suspicious. Of what, Seamus couldn't be sure, until his oldest daughter added, acidly, "Or our new nanny."

"Seamus." Kurt had spotted them. Tall, gray-haired, unpolished, he joined Seamus and held out his hand. "Roads clear?"

"Not bad. Snow-packed on the pass. The usual. You've met my daughter, Lauren."

"I think she was a few heads shorter back then. Nice to see you." Kurt shook Lauren's hand. "Where are you in school?"

Very politic, Seamus observed, as Kurt knew Lauren's age.

"Still in high school," she said, taking the implied compliment—that she was perhaps a college student—in stride.

"In the Sultan Mountain School, no less." Seamus smiled at his friend, now recognizing traces of Rory in Kurt's features. "We met your daughter."

"Where is she?"

Any disapproval was well-concealed, yet Seamus wondered if it was there, nonetheless. Father-daughter tensions? Kurt had high standards—for himself and others.

"She went to feed her snake," Lauren said.

"Her roommate's," Seamus corrected, as if it were important.

"Ah." Kurt made no further comment.

"And she's coming back to take us to the house."

The front door swung open, and Rory came in, curls flying loose from her ponytail, expression mildly agitated. "Hi. Ready to go?" she asked without preamble.

Seamus wondered if Rory was trying to avoid her father's notice for some reason.

Kurt seemed to sense it, too. "Everything all right?" he asked mildly.

"Yes." A tight smile. "And here?"

Kurt nodded.

The phone rang, and a young man behind the hotel's old reception counter picked it up. "Sultan Mountain School," he said. Then, "She's here. Rory, it's for you. It's Desert."

Irritated, Rory walked to the phone and said, "Hello?"

"When are you going to be able to practice? We're planning to do our new combo with the staffs on Friday, and we still don't have it right."

"I'm at work now, Desert."

"This is a responsibility, too."

Rory taught belly dance and fire-dancing at workshops approximately once a month and gave two students weekly private lessons. The troupe was a commitment she'd made, but it wasn't a job. "I can't talk now. I'll see you later."

"Well…okay."

Kurt turned away from Seamus Lee and his family, saying, "Let me know if you need anything."

CHAPTER TWO

THEY SAT IN the living room of the Empire Street house. That is, Lauren sat at the dining room table filling out a questionnaire regarding her personal goals in connection to the Sultan Mountain School, while Seamus did the same at the coffee table. Caleb was already off with a group of kids his own age at a snowboarding class, and Belle was in the next room happily watching a video. Rory sounded out Beau on what he wanted from the school, on his interests. Seuss, the puppy, lay in his crate, head tilted to one side.

Seamus heard Rory say to Beau, "Part of our curriculum requires involvement with the local economy. This means doing something like a job. I have one possibility that's really the ultimate spot, you know? But I can only give it to somebody trustworthy, who respects the need for confidentiality. You have to be prepared to act like an adult. I figured because of the work your dad does, you might understand and be able to do that."

Seamus couldn't stop himself from glancing in their direction. Beau was sitting on a Victorian footstool and Rory occupied the end of a fainting couch. The teenager's gaze was focused on the floor. Janine had been blond, but only Lauren had inherited her coloring. The boys all had dark brown hair, like his, and so did Belle.

Without looking up, Beau asked, "What is it?"

"It's working for a woman who makes custom skis. This is a highly competitive industry, and designs and manufacturing methods are closely held secrets. But she's agreed to take on a Sultan Mountain School student. With your background in math and science, you might be some real help to her."

"Okay," Beau said, still not lifting his head.

Rory felt Seamus Lee's eyes on her. She already knew he found her interesting as a woman. It was clear in the way he looked at her and in his behavior toward her. She found him attractive, as well, but that was beside the point. Seamus was a participant in the Sultan Mountain School, and she mustn't offend him, or worse, become entangled with him. The latter would certainly cause her father to brand her unprofessional and she didn't need that.

She wasn't keen for a relationship, in any event. Though she'd had more success keeping boyfriends than holding a job, the men she'd been closest to inevitably had disappointed her. She was tired of men who considered skiing as much as possible to be a life goal. They seemed, well, immature. Seamus Lee, being a father, being the person he seemed to be, was probably relatively mature. He had a real life, and a significant vocation as an artist. And any success whatsoever at raising his children meant that he thought of someone other than himself at least part of the time.

She liked this man for spending time with his children, for knowing his children.

But his interest in her just now was inconvenient.

And she had already begun to wonder exactly what his relationship with his children was like. In her presence, he'd revealed his ignorance of the name of his youngest daughter's stuffed animal. To Rory, Belle had introduced her "stuffy," as she called it, as Mouse. Either she'd never bothered to tell her father its name, or he'd forgotten.

They were like a family, and not. The children seemed to tiptoe around Seamus, seemed to want to please him, and yet…well, it was a bit strange, that was all.

In any case, she'd never experienced a truly successful parent-child relationship. Her parents' marriage had been brief and it was still a mystery to her. And, well, her grandmother was one way and her mother had been another, and her father was different, still.

Rory knew that her mother had been athletic, as her father was, and comfortable in the outdoors. Her grandmother said that Rory's mother had been into everything natural. Rory thought she herself was probably more like Gran. Gran had been a lounge singer, had worked on cruise ships, had been worshipped by many men—admittedly, Rory hadn't yet experienced that—and was a true free spirit. Rory's mother, Kristin Nichols Gorenzi, had died after skiing into a tree. Rory's father hadn't been there. Another man had—her mother's lover. Gran had told Rory this.

Rory's mother had been pretty, small and blond, with a bright, wide smile. Rory couldn't even *imagine* what her mother had been like. But she could believe that the fact she'd died while skiing with another man had helped drive Kurt Gorenzi from his daughter's life.

"Why don't I call the ski shop," Rory said to Beau, "and if the owner's keen, I'll take you over tomorrow to meet her. She has one other employee. He's college age, and he's really nice. He actually helps my fire-dancing troupe a lot."

"Your *what?*"

It was Seamus who'd spoken. Rory glanced up. His green eyes were long-lashed, and his sharp, elegant features and wavy long black hair reminded her of Viggo Mortensen in *The Lord of the Rings*.

"Oh, my roommates and I are fire dancers. Actually, we belly dance, too. It's both. We call it fire fusion. Our troupe is named Caldera."

Seamus continued to gaze at her intently, as if he were trying to see inside her. "A woman of unusual talents. How did you get into that?"

"In college… Well, when I was in college—" another failed enterprise "—I saw a troupe perform. And then I took some classes and I was hooked. I actually preferred belly dance and fire-dancing to school."

The puppy cried and Beau stood up. "I'll take him out."

"Thank you, son," his father said and forced his eyes back to his questionnaire.

Again, Rory caught it—that hungry look, this time on Beau's face. It was a hunger for words from his father, *anything* resembling attention from his father.

"What exactly do you do with fire?" Seamus asked.

"Poi and staff twirling. Poi are balls that are attached to tethers—cords. We swing them in patterns, making them go around each other. It's fun. Poi comes from New Zealand, originally, and fire-dancing is practiced all over the world. The belly dance we do is called American Tribal Style, which was developed by a woman in San Francisco."

"Aren't you afraid of being burned?" asked Seamus, abandoning his questionnaire entirely.

I'm perplexed by how little attention this

man is paying to his kids. What is wrong with him? Obviously, her original assessment of him as an involved father had been somewhat off the mark. She was reminded of her own father; and, consequently, she felt for the Lee children.

"Well—I've been burned. It happens." She pulled up her sleeves to display minor scars on her forearms. "We try to avoid it. And we're extremely good at first aid. But we practice and practice and practice, repeatedly, without fire, before we *ever* light up."

Seamus tried to shift his attention away from Rory's heart-shaped face, which struck him as elfin and mysterious. *She plays with fire....*

Too much like Janine.

But completely *unlike* his wife, too.

Because he could tell that Rory wasn't a boaster. She was clearly...just Rory. Already, he felt completely at ease in her presence.

Beau had opened Seuss's crate, and the puppy rushed out, wiggling all over. He jumped on Beau and the boy petted him enthusiastically.

"Don't do that," Rory said before she could

stop herself. *Engage brain,* then *mouth,* she reminded herself too late.

"Why not?" Seamus asked.

"Because soon that dog's going to be eighty pounds or more, and you don't want anything that size jumping on people. So don't reward him with attention for it now."

Beau looked up at her, with his father's eyes. He stopped petting the puppy and tried to hold him by his collar.

The puppy's lead lay on top of the crate, and Beau fastened it to his collar. They headed out the front door.

Seamus gazed at the questionnaire. *What are you hoping to get from your experience at the Sultan Mountain School?*

He bent over the coffee table and wrote, *I'm doing this for my kids. I want to get them away from Telluride, from the atmosphere of entitlement there. I want them to live someplace where things are a bit different and to understand that they're not better than other people, just luckier than most of them. Maybe I should've taken them to Rio de Janeiro instead, to the* favelas. *But I thought a town here that hasn't yet been spoiled by money might be the answer. For myself, I'd like to feel more competent in the outdoors and more aware of my environment. Some avalanche knowledge would also be a good thing.*

The next question: *Anything special you'd like to do during your time at the Sultan Mountain School?*

He reminded himself that Kurt might read his answer. *See Rory Gorenzi fire dance,* wouldn't be the most tactful response. He wrote, *Surprise me,* and then put down his pen.

Lauren finished filling out her questionnaire, brought it to Rory and sat down on a stiff velvet couch.

"Well, he'll be good protection," Seamus finally said, thinking about the dog.

Rory reminded herself that saying too much tended to get her in trouble. But she *had* to say this. "Actually, that's one of the biggest misunderstandings people have about dogs. In truth, we protect them. We're their *only* protectors. Yes, a trained protection dog can bite and hold on to an assailant. And, yes, some people will think twice about messing with you, if you're accompanied by a big, powerful dog. But our role with all pets is that of *their* protector. The best way to protect dogs is by obedience training them." As she spoke, Rory thought of Lola. Yes, in taking Lola into her home and her life, Desert had agreed to be the snake's protector. It didn't matter that Lola was a reptile and would never have a special attachment to Desert, and that the python might kill any of them randomly, for reasons unknown to them.

Rory turned her attention to Lauren Lee. The girl was tall, coltish and blond. She carried herself in a way that suggested she was used to being admired, used to popularity.

Rory picked up her questionnaire, skimming the answers.

Since I'm here, I'd like to improve my snowboarding, progress into backcountry snowboarding, become more self-sufficient.

Since I'm here?

Lauren, perhaps, would have preferred to remain in Telluride.

"Tomorrow," Rory said, "avalanche conditions willing, you and I can go up to Colorado Bowl and snowboard."

"You snowboard?" Lauren asked, possibly the longest sentence she'd yet uttered to Rory.

"I do. We'll snowshoe up, packing our

boards. Why don't you have your stuff together at eight? We'll check our packs to make sure we have everything."

THAT EVENING, WHILE Beau stayed with Caleb and Belle, Seamus and Lauren walked the puppy around the block and returned through the alley between their house and what turned out to be Rory Gorenzi's home. Seamus knew where they were when he and Lauren saw swirling fire inside the pink house's chain-link fence. The fire seemed to streak through the air as three women made tethered fireballs swing and arc around each other. The young man Seamus had seen that morning at the Sultan Mountain School sat drumming. He was dressed for frigid weather, but his hands were covered only with thin fingerless gloves. The women wore winter athletic tights and jackets, and their heads were covered with hats.

Their walk had been quiet, with observations related to air temperature (frigid), the amount of ice on the streets (lots), and Seuss's strength (considerable). A conversation for strangers. Seamus *knew* his daughter—and yet he didn't. They lived in the same house, and yet their paths almost never crossed.

Elizabeth's right, he thought. *I don't know them.*

It had always seemed right for his children to have full schedules. Lauren spent many weekends and summers away at camps— soccer camp, dance camp, cheerleading camp. So did the others, all but Belle, and Belle had a nanny. They all, of course, had Fiona, too, that remarkable woman who had entered their lives like Mary Poppins the year before Janine's death. The children all had Fiona, always.

Except at the moment.

His name's Mouse, Belle had told Rory. *He's a stuffy.*

Stuffy. How long since he'd heard that word? Belle must have learned it from Lauren. The kids were much closer to each other than they were to him. Protective of each other, as well.

Lauren gazed at the three fire-spinners. "I'd like to do that."

Seamus thought it looked dangerous and remembered what Rory had said about getting burned. But he didn't discourage his daughter. Hadn't he brought the children to Sultan to embrace a different lifestyle? Though, of course, there must be a fire dancer or two in Telluride. Certainly, such troupes had performed there.

Janine would have wanted to try spinning poi, just to prove she could and that she wasn't afraid. Everything she did was intended to illustrate her strength, her independence.

Including the gun.

Seamus and Lauren lingered at the fence, watching. Seamus's mind shifted to Ki-Rin, to the character he had created—the character who was his livelihood. He could easily develop an anime character like Rory to fit into the world of Ki-Rin. Perhaps a fire goddess of some kind... Ten cold minutes later, the women finished dancing and extinguished their poi.

Rory glanced up and saw them. She walked over to the fence.

Seamus said, "Very impressive."

"It was a good practice. Everything went right."

"Can we hope for a glimpse of the snake?" he asked.

"Beau would be disappointed," Rory told him, "if you got to see Lola and he didn't."

Of course, she was right. Understanding his kids better than he did.

She told Lauren, "*I* better get to bed, so I'm ready for snowboarding tomorrow." And to Seamus, she said, "You'll be starting avalanche school. It will be a four-day session, with classroom activities in the morning and field practice in the afternoon."

"The kids should have it, too," he remarked. "At least, Lauren and Beau."

"They will. Just not on the same schedule as you."

Watching her smile, Seamus wondered if she had some surprise up her sleeve. "I thought you would be teaching all of us," he said.

"I will—on different days. All the instructors rotate. I'm your program coordinator." Her breath steamed as she spoke, and Seamus thought again how pretty she was.

There was no reason for his attraction to Rory Gorenzi to feel so inappropriate. Except that this was the first extended amount of time he'd spent with his children—all of them together—since Janine's death. He feared that the temptation to pursue Rory was just another way to avoid their company.

I need to avoid them.

He had found Janine after the accident. Forensic evidence had proved that neither he, nor anyone else, had killed her—and had established that it wasn't suicide.

No way would it have been suicide, in any case. Janine would never have taken that way out, and she hadn't wanted to go.

It had been an accident. A stupid accident. Because she'd decided she needed to carry a gun. Because she'd *wanted* to carry one. Because she'd needed to prove to the world how tough she was.

The anger simmered within him all over again, and he tried to block it out. And hoped that none of his children would mention the subject of their mother for the next three months.

"I WANT FIONA!"

Belle's sobs were something Seamus hadn't anticipated. Even less had he anticipated that his own daughter would not be comforted by his arms.

Lauren reached for her. "Baby Belle, it's

okay. Look. You're upsetting Mouse. He's going to cry, too."

"He misses Fiona!" Belle said.

Seamus thought in amazement of the slim, sure elderly woman now kayaking in Baja. Fiona, with her long white braid and her love of poetry and opera and ballet and openness to learning about all that was new.

Seamus surrendered Belle to his oldest daughter. The four-year-old turned and gazed at him with what looked like a combination of suspicion and curiosity. He could still smell the child scent of her and marveled that it should seem foreign to him, instead of familiar.

"Mouse wants you to sleep with us," Belle told Lauren. "Please."

Seamus's reaction was to forbid it, on the impulse that Belle should be taught independence. Then, as if from long ago, he remembered the fears of his other children when they were younger, back in the days when he *had* known them. He would have to be a monster not to want this child, with her small tear-streaked face, to feel safe and comforted.

"Is it okay?" Lauren asked hesitantly, looking at him.

He realized that she didn't call him Dad. She didn't call him anything. "Of course."

Lauren smiled and told Belle, "We can't let Mouse feel lonely. I'll sleep in the other bed." She nodded to the room's second twin. "We'll share. Okay, baby?"

"Mouse loves you," Belle told her sister.

CHAPTER THREE

EARLY THE NEXT MORNING, Rory and Lauren strapped on snowshoes over their snowboarding boots. They carried packs made by CamelBak, with water reservoirs, as well as emergency blankets, and small first-aid kits. Rory also wore an avalanche beacon and carried her shovel in her pack, though they were not going into any avalanche zone.

"This looks pretty tame," Lauren pointed out, although she was breathing hard from the hike uphill.

"Good. We're just starting out with this. The country around here has a lot of avalanche danger, so I don't want to take you anywhere hairier until you've gone through the course and learned to use a beacon."

"I wish I could take a course in fire-dancing," Lauren said.

"I don't know how your dad would feel about that. And I've never taught a minor with fire. Of course, you don't actually *learn* twirling or poi with fire. You learn without. It's essential to practice for months, to get really good, before you bring fire into it."

"I'd practice without fire," Lauren told her. "But I'm not afraid of fire."

Rory glanced at her, noting the remark. She turned the comment over in her mind, knowing it would have relevance to snowboarding and everything else this girl did.

"I am," Rory said. "I'm afraid of getting burned and I'm afraid of breaking bones snowboarding and skiing, and I'm afraid of being buried in an avalanche. It doesn't stop me doing any of the things I like to do, but it does make me determined to do things the right way. Fear is what helps us stay alive."

"I guess," Lauren said without conviction. "Our family's not fearful, though. I'm not, in any case."

Why did she point that out? Rory wondered. What was wrong with a little healthy fear?

They made the run together, Rory following Lauren. Lauren was obviously an accomplished snowboarder. Her form was excellent.

Probably, she'd had the best teachers in Telluride.

Rory led her up another slope, breathing hard as she made her way over the powder in her snowshoes. They snowboarded together for three hours, then headed back to the Empire Street house in Rory's car, a black Toyota RAV4 that she'd bought used. As they turned down Main Street, however, Rory spotted a familiar shape wearing a day pack and walking with the help of an ornately curved walking stick. Her grandmother wore black wool pants and an imitation ermine coat, and her still-thick white hair was swept up in a French twist beneath her matching fake fur hat.

Snow fell heavily as Rory pulled up beside her and rolled down the window. "Gran, do you want a ride?"

"Of course not, Rory." Her mother's mother frowned with interest at Lauren. "I will fall apart if I don't keep up with my walking."

Walking, dancing, singing, yoga, Rory filled in. The way Sondra had raised her—good grief, she'd learned to ski by being guided down slopes between her grandmother's legs—seemed to have determined that she pursue an active, healthy lifestyle. Part of her love of fire-dancing and belly dance had come from her grandmother's enthusiasm when she'd learned of Rory's new interests; without being told, Sondra had seemed to understand that what Rory liked was the peaceful concentration required to work with fire.

Feeling a surge of love for Sondra, Rory told the woman, "This is one of my dad's clients, Lauren Lee. This is Sondra Nichols," she told Lauren, "my grandmother."

"It's nice to meet you," Lauren said dutifully.

As they went on their way, Lauren asked, "Is your grandfather alive, too?"

"No. He died before I was born. She's been widowed thirty-five years, and as long as I can remember, she's always said that she'll never marry again."

"Like my dad."

Rory glanced over in interest.

Lauren said, "He has girlfriends, of course. In fact, don't be surprised if he tries to make you the next one. But he never marries them."

Rory couldn't read the teenager's tone— not with accuracy. "Do you wish he would?"

"I don't really care," Lauren said. "It's not like he has that much to do with us, anyhow."

The reply shocked Rory, and bothered her. She knew what it was to have a father who didn't "have that much to do" with her. She'd never held it against her father, believing he was devastated by her mother's death—and by her betrayal. But in Seamus Lee, who had four children, one of them just four years old, noninvolvement seemed criminal.

"I thought he had the kind of job…" Rory stopped abruptly.

"Oh, he *could* spend time with us. And he used to, before my mom died. But not anymore."

"How did your mother die?" Reflecting that she and the Lee children shared motherless status, Rory pulled up outside the Lees' temporary home. Lights were on inside, illuminating the Greek Revival house against the gray afternoon, making it warm and welcoming.

"A handgun accident. The forensic people figured she was loading it and didn't know it was already loaded or something like that. I don't really know how handguns work."

Neither did Rory. She wondered why Seamus Lee's wife had been loading a handgun in the first place.

"She didn't put up with anything from anyone," Lauren said.

Assertiveness through firearms? thought Rory. No fear, handguns... There was something amiss with this family, but she couldn't put her finger on it.

And it's none of your business, anyhow.

Rory longed to ask *why*—about the handgun—but it seemed a delicate question to put to this girl. Instead, she said, "I want to get you into an avalanche class as soon as possible. But, in the meantime, how would you feel about teaching snowboarding to kids at the ski area?"

"To little kids?"

"Yes."

"All right." Lauren seemed to be thinking it over. "I could do that."

"I think you could, too," Rory agreed.

"What about fire-dancing?" she asked Rory. "Can you teach me?"

"Without fire. Possibly so. Let me look into it."

Leaving Lauren at the house, Rory drove out to San Juan Ski and Snowboard to check on Beau and see how he was getting along in his new part-time job. She found him happily learning to use a jigsaw and not at all keen to return to Empire Street. Nonetheless, he was in an afternoon telemark class.

Telemark, an old form of free-heel skiing, allowed the skier freedom from the necessity of chairlifts and greater access to the backcountry. The style of skiing emphasized controlled turns, the proper execution of which was an art form.

Gigi Parks, the ski designer, pulled a pair of telemark skis off the wall and pushed them in Beau's direction. "Give these a try and tell me what you think."

Her assistant, Rory's friend Woody, called goodbye to Beau as he and Rory left.

Rory was still preoccupied by the fact that the children's mother had died in a handgun accident. She wanted to know the facts, and there was only one family member she could ask. The two of *them* had time booked for an hour of telemarking that afternoon, after he finished avalanche school.

Beau broke into her thoughts. "I like that place. I feel like I'm learning to do something *useful*."

Rory considered this remark. "I'm glad you like it. I thought that might be a good fit for you."

"Is it a group telemark class?"

"I think there are two other students." She braked at a stop sign, then glanced over at him. "Is that okay?"

"I hate group lessons."

Rory didn't ask why. When people said that, there was usually one reason: fear of ridicule.

"Try it today," she said, "and I'll check with you tonight and see how it went. If it's no good for you, we might be able to manage a solo lesson or two."

The look he shot her was one of naked gratitude.

What a group these children were.

On Empire Street, Rory found Caleb outside on a snowskate. The seven-year-old was clearly a skateboarder. The snowskate consisted of a skateboard deck balanced on a short, wide ski, creating something that was a cross between snowboard and skateboard and perfect for transportation on Sultan's icy streets.

However, Caleb was not wearing a helmet,

and this wouldn't fly with her. "Where's your dad?" she asked as she got out of the car.

"He's not back from avalanche school yet. Lauren's watching us."

"Well, you need to have a helmet on, Caleb."

He made a face that promised lack of cooperation. "I don't have to," he said. "I don't fall."

"Congratulations on not falling, but while you're here in Sultan, you're learning safety from the Sultan Mountain School. That means wearing a helmet."

"It's *my* snowskate."

"And no one makes you wear a helmet at home?"

He'd clearly been caught out. He glared at Rory and stalked inside. Caleb might turn out to be the rebel of this lot, she thought. He wore his hair below his shoulders, and even at seven he had the confidence of someone who knew himself to be a capable athlete.

Rory followed Beau inside the house and found Lauren rubbing the German shepherd puppy's nose in a puddle on the floor. Lauren started to drag the dog back to his crate, and Rory said, "Actually, what you want to do now is take him outside to wherever you want him to pee. Then, you've got to clean up with carpet stuff that will neutralize the pheromones. There's some in the cupboard beside the sink."

Lauren cast her a look that seemed to weigh all these instructions. She said, "Beau, take Seuss outside. You have your boots on already."

Beau grabbed the leash and said, "What am I supposed to do?"

Teaching children how to train their puppy was beyond the call of duty, and Rory had hoped to grab a snack before telemarking with Seamus Lee. Instead, she gave the two siblings better ideas for corrections than "rub his nose in it," made sure Caleb was wearing his snowboarding helmet and instructed Lauren and Beau that this was strict school policy.

THIS TIME, THEY took his car and drove to the head of a trail and out onto a long, gentle slope where they could practice turns.

Rory remembered how determined she was to know more about the handgun, but there were too many other things to attend to in the meantime. First—Caleb and the helmet.

"He knows he's to wear a helmet," Seamus said. "The woman who works for me always makes him wear one. She's an older lady who, well, runs my household, if you will. She's something of a renaissance woman. If my kids have any good values, it's because of her."

"Good values, such as…?"

"Well, she has many interests. She loves ballet and poetry. She gets them reading classics and has actually gotten them listening to opera, at times. And, of course, she encourages them to spend time outdoors. Climbing trees, skiing. Enjoying nature. And she's gotten Beau to do some writing. She's kayaking in Baja right now."

"It sounds as though you're fortunate to have her working for you," Rory said carefully.

"Yes." Seamus fell silent, frowning as he considered the road ahead.

Lauren tells me your wife died in an accident with a handgun. As Rory played this over in her mind, she knew she could not put it to him that way. Feigning ignorance? Yes, that was best. "Are you divorced?"

"No, my wife passed away when Belle was one."

"I'm sorry. How did she die?" Rory hated the fact that her need to know the why of the handgun was stronger than any wish to save this man the pain of discussing his wife's death.

"She was checking her handgun and it fired, and she was hit by a ricocheting bullet. At least, that's what the forensic experts thought."

"Was this in Telluride?"

"Yes, believe it or not. Janine represented battered women, and she'd been threatened by some of her clients' spouses. So, she took to carrying a gun. It wasn't..." He stopped.

Rory glanced at him, her eyes lingering on his cleft chin. He was a mystery, and she felt her interest piqued by what she could not reach within him.

He didn't continue, so she finished the thought for him. "It wasn't what you would have done?"

"No. It wasn't."

Rory didn't know how to convey what she needed to get across. *Maybe you don't need to say it, Rory. Saying too much is what gets you in trouble.* But there was nothing *bad* about what she wanted to say. "Lauren seems utterly fearless."

"Nobody's utterly fearless."

The man was remote, Rory decided. Why? Possibly, Seamus Lee was simply unfriendly and uninterested in his children. But hadn't Lauren said that he used to be different before his wife had died?

"I apologize for bringing up a painful subject," she said at last.

"It's better you know," he replied shortly. "You're spending time with my kids, after all."

They spoke little after that. Rory directed him to a turnout near the trailhead, and they climbed out of his SUV and snugged up their boots and put on their skis. "You've telemarked before," Rory clarified.

"Not as much as I'd like. My work is time-consuming."

"Can you make a tele turn?" she asked.

"Barely."

She grinned. "Just so we know where we're starting." It occurred to her that rather than putting Beau in a group telemark class, she could teach him and his father together. That would let Beau spend some time with his dad—and probably relax many of his fears about group classes.

They put skins on their skis—adhesive cloth trimmed to the dimensions of each ski. Skins allowed the skis to glide forward but kept them from sliding backward, making it possible for the skier to climb slopes.

Seamus followed Rory as she started up the route she'd chosen, onto a steeply climbing trail. She moved confidently, as he painfully remembered skiing with Janine. As soon as the memory surfaced, the anger came, too. He saw in his mind her pugnacious jaw, heard her voice and her conversation, scattered with surfing and snowboarding slang. Her tough act. He'd been attracted to her in part because of the vulnerability he'd been certain lay beneath that tough exterior. He'd seen a wounded woman with a wounded child trapped inside, and he'd never stopped wanting to reach the vulnerable person beneath.

And he *had* reached her. But seldom. And by then, too, he'd known better than to let her know what he'd seen.

Lauren seems fearless.

He'd known that what Rory had said was not what she believed. Rory had seen Lauren repeating her mother's tough act. And she'd seen something amiss, as he did. Did Rory have any idea what to do with a teenager who had chosen self-destructive toughness as her guide in life?

Because the real Lauren was not that tough. She was the loving older sister who gave up her own room to make sure Belle felt safe at night. After he'd said good night to Lauren and Belle the night before, when he was lying alone in the double bed in the master suite, he'd realized he should have praised Lauren for her kindness to Belle.

They climbed the trail for a mile, and Seamus began to wonder when Rory would stop and if he'd have to ask her to take a break. But suddenly she slowed, turned her skis slightly and looked at him. "Still breathing?" she asked with a grin.

It was not Janine's type of challenging grin, the kind of grin that noted her own athletic superiority. Rory's grin seemed more like an invitation to have fun; a way of saying, It's downhill all the way now and you're going to love it, and so will I.

"Breathing hard," he admitted.

"Let's put our skins away and have some water," Rory suggested. "Then, we can make some turns."

Seamus studied the slope she'd chosen, leading off the trail and ending in a gentle bowl.

"Are we agreed," Rory said, "that it's better to be safe than speedy?"

"We're agreed."

"Are you comfortable with this slope?"

"It looks perfect for my level."

She nodded with satisfaction. The sun had come out and they peeled the skins off their skis, stowed them and stood in the afternoon sun, drinking water. Then, Rory suggested, "I'd like you to go first, if you're comfortable with that."

She gave him a few pointers, advising him to let his skis choose the most natural course and to slow himself *before* he found that he was going too fast.

Impressed with her guidance, Seamus pushed off, following the instructions, letting his skis pick the fall line and remembering advice he'd received in previous telemark classes. He made two not-very-pretty turns and pulled up on the edge of the slope in the shade of the trees to watch Rory descend.

She skied gracefully, seeming part of the snow, one with her skis, her motion fitted exactly to the terrain.

When she stopped, he said, "You're good. Did your dad teach you?"

She wore sunglasses, but he felt the intensity of the gaze behind them as she looked at him. "No," she replied. For a moment, he thought she was going to add something, but instead she spoke to him about keeping his weight forward and also about letting the distribution of weight on his skis make each turn for him.

They skied together, and there was an immense and peaceful quiet in the snow and trees, with the mountains above them. Though he was more tired physically than he could remember being for months, Seamus also felt rested. What was more, he was looking forward to returning to the Empire Street house and seeing his children.

At the bottom of one run, Rory realized he was gazing at her intently. "What?"

"I want to put you into Ki-Rin's world," he said.

Rory blinked, remembering his vocation.

"Each of my children has a character," he said. "In Ki-Rin's world."

"That's beautiful," she exclaimed, trying to downplay the implications of his making a character for *her*. The thought made her feel warm, set her off-balance. *This can't happen,* she thought. *The job, Rory. Keep your job.*

WHEN THEY RETURNED to the car, Seamus put their skis on the overhead rack. Rory, he noticed, didn't object to the courtesy. He turned to find her watching him and she immediately blushed and turned away.

Seamus felt a small smile forming on his lips. "We're making pizza tonight. Would you like to join us? If you've had enough of the Lee family, I understand, but it would be great to have you."

Rory checked her watch without glancing at him again. "I teach a class at six. Belly dance and fire dance. By the way, your daughter has asked to learn fire dance, and I could teach her to spin poi and twirl staffs *without* anything on fire. You'd have to come with her to the Sultan Recreation Center and sign a release."

Seamus pondered Lauren's sometimes tough act, which reminded him of Janine at her worst. Would the activities Rory was referring to increase his daughter's need to prove that she was fearless? "Without fire," he repeated.

"Yes. I never teach with fire this time of year, anyhow. We don't have a facility in town that is insured for it. But, in any case, Lauren would need lots of practice before that stage."

"She's not reckless," he admitted, almost as though arguing a point—though with whom he couldn't have said. "Sure. I'll come and sign the waiver, and you can bring her back afterward and join us for pizza. How long does the class last?"

"Till seven-thirty. Half of it is belly dance. The other half is poi spinning and staff twirling."

INCLUDING LAUREN, RORY had four students. It seemed a small class, but Sultan was a small, remote town. Though tourism was reviving the local economy, Seamus could tell from its sleepy winter streets that Sultan still struggled. He signed Lauren's waiver and then headed back home, where Beau was watching Caleb and Belle during his brief absence.

The Sultan Mountain School provided day care for Belle when Seamus couldn't be with her and when she wasn't in ski school. At four years of age, she couldn't be expected to be outside or in classes all day. Tomorrow, he knew, Rory would supervise Lauren teaching his youngest daughter's ski class. He saw the pitfalls of this already. Belle would cling to Lauren and make it impossible for her to work with the other children in the class.

Not my problem. He felt guilty for the thought. If his children caused trouble, it *was* his problem.

When he got home, he checked the pizza dough, which Beau had kneaded in his absence. Half an hour before Rory and Lauren were due back, he and Beau put the dough onto two pizza pans and began assembling toppings. Belle was playing on the floor in the other room with Caleb and the puppy.

From the kitchen, Seamus heard her shriek and then howl.

He hurried to the living room, Beau right behind him, and found Belle hugging herself and sobbing, "He bit me!" Seuss was cowering under the dining table.

Seamus saw, with something like horror, that indeed there was a small puncture mark on his daughter's arm.

"You were bugging him!" Caleb said.

Seamus didn't know what to do about a puppy bite. What if this meant he had a vicious dog on his hands?

He said, "Let's put Seuss in his crate." He walked to the dining room table and scooped the puppy from beneath it.

Seuss looked as if he didn't understand at all what it was that he'd done.

Seamus reached for Belle and picked her up. *I've hardly held this child,* he thought, as he had so many times in the past forty-eight hours, since Fiona had left for Baja. "Now, calm down and tell me what happened. Then, we'll wash off your arm."

Belle's sobs became hiccups and finally stopped. Seamus examined the bite again. Just one tiny puncture wound. Did he need to take her to the clinic? It was an animal bite, after all. Seuss had received all his shots, but still…

"He probably was teething on her," Beau

said. "He does that to me a lot." He held out his hand and pointed to a small scab. "His teeth are sharp. They're puppy teeth, and that's why they're so sharp."

Seamus wondered what his son's authority was for this statement.

Caleb said, "Belle was climbing around and jumping over Seuss and stuff, and he was excited, and he growled a little and bit her. It looked like he was playing."

"He probably was," Beau said.

"Well, let's go wash your arm, Belle," Seamus decided.

He was just applying a Band-Aid when the front door opened.

Belle followed her father down the hall to the front room. "Lauren, Seuss bit me!"

"He did what?" Lauren asked.

Rory sank down on the couch to listen to the story of the puppy bite.

Seamus turned to her. "Should I take her to the clinic?"

Rory eyed the wound, which Belle was showing Lauren, and shook her head. She was exhausted, and hungry, but she couldn't ignore the situation that had presented itself.

Seamus Lee had chosen to acquire a dog

that would grow to be large and powerful. That meant he was going to have to train the dog *and* his children, and he was going to have to supervise his children with the dog during the process.

Dog training is not part of my job description, she thought with some irritation.

But could she turn her back on this?

She remembered Gandalf.

She could not stand to see such a dog ruined by not receiving the training he needed. So many dogs ended their lives in shelters because no one had helped them learn rules for living with people.

"He needs to be in obedience class," she said.

"There probably isn't one in Sultan," Seamus remarked. "Is there?"

I can't do it all. I can't do everything! But she probably knew more about German shepherds than anyone else in Sultan. "I'll see what I can find out. Look, all of you have to discourage him from chewing on people. He probably nipped Belle, and those milk teeth are sharp."

"Like I said," Beau put in.

"Here, let's let him out." She sat on the

floor and opened the crate. The puppy tumbled out, scrambling into her lap. He began licking her hands, then teething on one of them. Rory firmly and gently closed his jaw with her hand, lifted his head so that his eyes met hers, and growled, soft and low. Then, she released him. When he sat comfortably in her lap again, she petted him and said, "Good boy." Briefly, she gave them some guidelines for correcting the puppy, then said, "But I'm not a dog trainer, and you need to take this puppy to school. I recommend *lots* of obedience lessons. Dogs usually like them, and the training helps all of you learn to be consistent. Also, it will help him get along with other dogs."

Seamus said ruefully, "I didn't realize a dog would be so much work."

She shouldn't say it. It was too opinionated. They wouldn't like her if she said it.

But she had to say it, because Seuss was a good puppy and had a chance of becoming a great dog. "If you're not prepared to put in the time, you should return him to the breeder. It's not fair to him, and you just can't have an animal like this and *not* train him."

"I'll train him," Beau said. "We're not taking him back. I'll train him."

While she would have doubted most children's long-term commitment to such a project, Rory believed him. There was a steadiness to Beau that she liked and admired. But she knew the conversation about the dog was not over. Someone also needed to speak to Seamus about supervising Seuss with his children and their playmates and with teaching his children how to treat the puppy.

Her instincts told her to stay out of the situation, to keep her mouth shut. But this wasn't for the usual reason—that saying too much tended to get her in trouble.

It was because, as Seamus Lee had put her skis on the car that day, she'd felt that mysterious whisper of being cared for, being looked after, being cherished. The whisper had suggested a future—an *imaginary* future, just happy thoughts in her mind, about a man like Seamus caring for her. Wanting to make a Ki-Rin character for her. Yet she couldn't afford to think that way, even casually. She wanted so badly to succeed at this job, to earn her father's esteem.

She needed to back off from Seamus Lee and his family—from their emotional lives.

Yet someone had to talk to him about the dog.

CHAPTER FOUR

EVEN BELLE WANTED to see Lola, the Burmese python, so after pizza the entire Lee family followed Rory back to her house. On the way, she considered how to segue from acknowledging the inappropriateness of a Burmese python in a household with children, to responsible dog ownership.

Stay out of it, Rory.

Samantha was working—she waited tables at one of the two restaurants in Sultan that remained open during the winter—but Desert was home. Rory found her housemate painting her toenails.

"Desert, these are some of SMS's new clients. Seamus Lee and his children—Lauren, Beau, Caleb and Belle. Seamus, everyone, this is Desert Katz. They've come to look at Lola."

Seamus watched as Desert stood up, her long flared pants skimming the Victorian floor, one of those authentic patterned floral floors, obviously restored with care. Rory's roommate's head was shaved; her skin bore many tattoos, and her nose, eyebrow and lip were all pierced. Ears, too.

She was beautiful—with model good looks, cheekbones, figure and all.

"Oh, I'll take you down," she said. "We can get her out."

"No," Rory said quickly. "We'll just look at her through the glass. Let's not bother her."

"She ate yesterday. She's going to be pretty lazy, in any case," Desert argued.

Rory shook her head, her expression clearly anxious.

Desert said, "Well, whatever. Come on downstairs."

The basement was lined with stone and surprisingly warm. Seamus noted that Rory kept close to her housemate—as if to prevent her from opening the large vivarium that stood in the center of the basement. It was a floor-to-ceiling unit—a glass room—and inside, a huge white-and-yellow snake with red eyes lay atop a boulder.

"Lola is an albino Burmese python," Rory said.

"Awesome," exclaimed Beau, coming closer.

"Would you like to hold her?" Desert asked.

"Sure!"

Rory said, "Actually, let's not."

"Don't be ridiculous," Desert told her.

"Desert, there are too many people here. It's too stressful for Lola."

Seamus said, "Beau, let's not do that."

"She's really gentle," Desert insisted.

Seamus could see that Rory was infuriated by her roommate's obstinate refusal to listen.

Rory faced his family. "Beau, the reason we're not taking Lola out is that she *is* a wild animal—a large one. She weighs around sixty pounds, and last summer she bit our other housemate and might have killed her if we hadn't been there. That's why we keep her safely inside her vivarium."

"She wouldn't have killed Samantha. She was just confused," Desert insisted.

Caleb said, "I want a snake, Dad. Not a big one. A little one."

Rory blinked and Seamus wondered why. But he, too, heard the strangeness of one of his children actually calling him Dad. Twenty-four hours around his family, and Rory had noticed that his own children were like strangers to him—and they treated him as a stranger.

"They're a fair amount of work," Rory said to Caleb. "But there are plenty of smaller snakes that make good pets. You definitely don't want one that will grow as big as Lola. But corn snakes are gentle and fairly inexpensive. Here, check out this book, Caleb." She went to a bookcase against one wall and selected a large colored encyclopedia of snakes.

Watching, Seamus felt enchanted—by her kindness toward his children, he supposed. Simply by her. She *was* pretty, but he had known more beautiful women. Her off-balance roommate, even, was more beautiful than Rory. But the roommate didn't have Rory's attentive presence, her instinctive caring—at least that was what he thought he saw in Rory Gorenzi. That when his children were present, her motivation was to listen, to attend, to care.

Desert seemed immature, in comparison to Rory—and less of the real world. He wondered why Rory lived with a woman like that, with a rather frightening zoo animal for a pet.

"What happened with your roommate?"

Lauren asked, gazing through the glass at the python.

"Well, Lola may not look like a lot of work, but it takes three of us to move her. We used to take turns feeding her, and then one day, we don't know why, she grabbed Samantha's leg and wouldn't let go. We didn't even know how to *make* her let go at that time. Now we keep some cold water ready in the refrigerator. We bring it out before we have to go into the enclosure. Supposedly, running cold water in her mouth will make her let go. Anyhow, Samantha needed stitches."

"It was that essential oil she was wearing," Desert insisted.

Rory shrugged. "Maybe. Anyway, now we never open the enclosure unless there are three adults present."

Belle stood beside Lauren and reached her arms up. "I don't like the big snake."

Seamus felt rejected by the preschooler and wasn't sure why. It was natural that Belle should turn to Lauren, since she knew her sister better than she knew him.

But before his oldest could pick up Belle, he himself raised her into his arms. Belle seemed momentarily surprised—and wary.

But then she leaned against him sleepily, gazing up at his face.

Watching, Rory smiled, and Seamus felt his heart leap. She was smiling at the two of them; at the sight of him with his youngest daughter.

Desert fell into step behind Seamus as he carried Belle upstairs, accompanied by the other children. Belle stared at Desert and asked, "Why don't you have hair?"

"I shave it off because I like how I look this way. Want to feel it?"

As they reached the kitchen, Belle stretched out a hesitant hand to touch Desert's head.

A young woman with glasses was just coming in the front door. "Oh, hi."

Seamus started, recognizing her face but unable to place it.

Rory introduced Seamus and his children to her second housemate, Samantha, who said to Seamus, "We've met. I interned as a legal aide at the Women's Resource Center one summer when your wife was there."

Ice chilled his veins. She'd known Janine.

"I thought I knew you," he managed to say.

Rory told his family, "Well, I'll see all of you tomorrow. Practice with your broom handle, Lauren, so you don't forget what we learned tonight."

Fire staff practice, Seamus thought, as his daughter smiled in response. The reminder of Janine faded away, leaving only a faint chill. Seamus guided his children out into the dark and the cold, but felt as if he was carrying some memory of warmth with him.

And perhaps that of Rory Gorenzi, too.

"YOU KNEW HIS WIFE?" Rory whispered the words, anxious they not be overheard by the people walking away on the other side of the door.

Samantha nodded with a sad half smile. "She was my boss."

"That's the summer you were in Telluride." And now Rory remembered Samantha returning to Sultan and saying her boss had been shot and had died, although she'd never said any more than that. Samantha had hated Telluride, though she'd liked the work. Rory was torn between demanding to know everything and showing a little restraint. *It's just morbid curiosity,* she thought. *Anyhow, Seamus already told me what happened.*

"What was she like?"

Samantha's blue eyes grew curious. "You like him?"

Rory waved a hand casually, indicating indifference.

Expression skeptical, Samantha said, "Well, Janine didn't talk about him much. In fact, I'd worked for her three weeks before I even knew she had kids. And she was nursing the littlest one then. When she talked about any of them, it was her oldest daughter; then her daughters, plural. So it was a while longer before I knew she had boys."

"What *did* she talk about?"

"Work. Batterers. Perps. Domestic terrorists, as she called them. Psychopaths, sociopaths. Big into psychology. Very... Almost masculine. Though I don't know why I'm saying that. She used slang a lot. Lots of profanity, too. She could be pretty abrasive, but she was also sweet with her clients. You got the feeling she'd been through some stuff herself somewhere in the past."

Rory considered that, weighing it with what Seamus had told her.

"Did she say *anything* about him?"

"Well, the gun was an issue. I mean, when I knew she was carrying it, I asked her if she was okay owning a gun with kids in the house. She said, 'Look, I don't let my husband tell me what to do.' Then, she went through all the safety precautions she used and said she was teaching her oldest daughter to shoot. And that girl must have been, like, ten. She also said, 'But we're not telling him. He doesn't get it.'"

I don't get it, either, Rory thought. Had Seamus ever learned that Lauren's mother had given her shooting lessons? "She must have been through an assault or something herself," she mused aloud.

"If she had been, she never told me. Janine was convinced this one client's ex-husband was insane and was going to kill her. I mean, he did threaten her, in pretty disgusting terms, and she had a restraining order against him. He *was* a scary guy."

Rory wondered if Seamus had been frightened for his wife. Or had he discounted her fear. Had the accident with the gun *been* an accident?

She bit back the thought as soon as it occurred. She'd never been assaulted, but growing up in Sultan and keeping her eyes open, working sometimes in lines of work traditionally reserved for men, she'd become streetwise—or, well, at least she wasn't totally naive. "How did she shoot herself?" Rory asked.

"It wasn't entirely certain, but the forensic evidence definitely pointed to an accident—and a fairly typical accident. It was nasty for Seamus for a while, because people knew they hadn't been getting along so well."

"They weren't getting along?"

"Well, the gun, at least, was an issue between them. He'd told her, 'Either the gun goes, or the children and I go.' I have no idea if he meant it. Gun-control people loved the outcome, of course."

Someone dying? Rory reflected. But she knew what Samantha meant. People interested in gun control could certainly point to the accident as proof that handgun ownership was dangerous.

The following morning, Rory told Beau that instead of going to the ski factory that day he would be joining his father in the afternoon for telemark lessons. In the morning, he and Lauren would be taking a tour of a local mine reclamation project.

"I don't want to telemark," he said.

"You wrote on your questionnaire that you do," Rory replied, frowning and wondering if she'd mixed up the family's answers.

"Well, I don't anymore. I'll snowboard."

They stood in the living room of the Lees' house. Rory had arrived to pick up Belle and Caleb for their morning ski lesson and to let the others know the plans for the day.

"Come on," Seamus said, downing his coffee. "It will be fun."

Caleb opened the front door and came in with the puppy on a leash.

Rory's heart constricted a little at the sight of Seuss. It was going to take a while to get over Gandalf's death. She wasn't sure whether the presence of a German shepherd puppy in her life would prove a hindrance or a help. She still hadn't spoken privately to Seamus about this dog.

It's not your job to talk to him about Seuss, she told herself again.

And, again, she concluded that she would say it, anyhow. *I'm going to say it even if it costs me this job.* There was no reason it should cost her the job, of course. And she had no idea how her father would feel about the situation.

Right now, however, she must focus on a different parent-child relationship. She wondered if Beau's relationship with *his* father was behind his sudden resistance to telemark lessons.

Beau said again, "I just want to snowboard."

Rory gave a small shake of her head and threw Beau a look she hoped was compassionate, but she held her ground. He was going to have a telemark lesson today.

The twelve-year-old acquiesced with a shrug.

Rory continued to explain the schedule for the day, then made sure the younger children had everything for their ski lesson. The SMS van arrived to take Beau and Lauren on the mine tour, and then Rory loaded Belle and Caleb in the backseat of her own car to drive them to the ski area. Seamus would walk to his avalanche class.

Fastening his seat belt, Caleb said, "Beau doesn't want to telemark because Dad never wants to take him."

Rory looked at him. Caleb had a sprinkle of freckles across his nose. His hair was as dark as his father's and overly long, and his eyes were a pale shade of aqua. When Caleb said no more, she replied, "Really?"

"He never wants to take us with him."

Belle, in her child seat, said, "Rory, can I learn to make the stick go around?"

Belle must be talking about staff twirling. She must have seen Lauren practicing with the broom handle Rory had given her. "I don't see why not," Rory answered. "But I'm pretty busy right now. Sometime when I'm not, we'll find a stick your size and I can show you how to twirl it."

"I like you," Belle said simply.

Warmth suffused Rory. "Thank you. I like you, too. Caleb, does Seuss know 'Sit' yet?"

He never wants to take us with him. As she drove the children to their ski lesson, she mulled over Caleb's revelations and the things Samantha had told her the night before about Seamus's wife, Janine, and her death. Janine Jensen.

Oh, she kept her maiden name, Samantha had said.

What troubled Rory the most was nothing the children or Seamus or Samantha had said. It was that now, after knowing him just two days, she seemed to have in her mind's eye details of Seamus—his cleft chin, his green eyes, the slight hollows in his cheeks, his jaw, the bass quality of his voice. She saw him so clearly. She saw him all the time, even when he wasn't there.

Something was creeping up on her, something bigger and more frightening than a simple instructor-client relationship. And she was spending far too much energy thinking about Seamus Lee.

AT NOON, WHILE walking back from the Sultan Mountain School to his house, Seamus phoned Telluride to check in with Elizabeth, who was supervising the studio in his absence. The first topic of conversation was Ki-Rin, Seamus's dragon-boy hero, who had provided so well for him and his family for so many years.

"Okay, so when he sees Koneko," Elizabeth said, "he transforms…"

"Not yet," Seamus interrupted. "She hasn't threatened him yet. He doesn't transform until she threatens him or someone else." The boy Ki-Rin would take on his dragon form only when that occurred. It annoyed Seamus slightly that Elizabeth hadn't yet picked up this fundamental aspect of the character. But there were other details to discuss related to the making of the latest Ki-Rin animated feature.

"How are you doing in Sultan?" Elizabeth asked at last.

"Good, good."

"Do your children remember who you are?"

Seamus could have done without the dig. In retrospect, he didn't like this woman, the last with whom he'd been involved. He liked her well enough as part of his studio team, but he didn't like the memories of dating her nearly as much.

"Fiona called," Elizabeth said. "Did she get you on your cell phone?"

"Actually, no. Is she all right?"

"Yes, but she's thinking of traveling some more with her son and his wife. Maybe she doesn't want to break it to you yet. You know what I mean."

"Yes." Fiona knew how he depended on her. But after only forty-eight hours without her... Well, it wasn't that he felt more able to cope with his children. He certainly still felt all the same anxieties when he was near them. Only the previous night, for instance, Lauren had told Beau that their mother had skied down Uncompahgre Peak one year. *She's skied down the backs of lots of these mountains.*

The resentment and anger had coursed through Seamus, and he'd gone outside so as not to have to hear, or comment on, what he'd heard.

Yes, Janine had been a good athlete.

Yes, she'd never let fear stop her from doing anything.

But she was… All the hard names for women came to his mind at the thought of her, at the thought of the handgun and the accident and…

And all of it.

And that reaction was the sole reason he had avoided spending time alone with his children since Janine's death. Because the compulsion to say everything going through his mind was almost beyond his control. And what would that do to them?

Nonetheless, when they weren't sharing their memories of Janine, Seamus found he *liked* being with his children.

And Rory Gorenzi, too.

He wanted to sort that out. Did he like her because of the children? Did he like his children's company only because of her? Was he using her as a friendly intermediary between himself and the kids?

It would be a mistake to become involved with any woman simply because she was good with his kids.

But it *had* been crazy for him to date women who didn't like to be with his children.

In any case, he wasn't going to have anything to do with Rory in that way. She was Kurt's daughter.

But he'd begun to count on her warmth, the easy caring she showed around his family. And he'd begun to see her clouds of hair, her wide smile and brown eyes, even when she wasn't with him.

He put away his phone as he neared the house.

Rory's car pulled up to the curb outside, and something lurched in his chest as she helped Belle out of one side of the backseat while Caleb scrambled out of the other. The front door of the house opened, and Seuss scrambled out. He slipped on some ice and rolled down the steps, and Rory, watching, erupted in laughter.

Beau came after the puppy, who was rushing toward the street. He ran, trying to catch him and chasing him into the road.

Rory, watching all this, set Belle on the sidewalk and ran toward the house, calling, "Seuss can't catch me, Seuss can't catch me."

Seamus reached them all as Rory, who had persuaded the puppy to chase her, caught the dog's collar and explained to Beau that you couldn't catch a puppy by running toward it. If the puppy ran into the street, they must run *away* and get the puppy to chase them back to the house.

Beau picked up Seuss. He was carrying the dog's leash. "I thought he would stay with me."

"He'll learn to," Rory said, "but he's still a baby."

Caleb ran to his father. "I'm the best skier in the class. I'm better than the instructor."

"I believe that," Seamus answered with a smile. Caleb had been skiing since he was three.

Rory said, "We'll be inside in a minute. I want to talk to your dad."

"I'm going to walk Seuss," Beau said and snapped the leash on the puppy's collar. He headed up the street toward the alley that separated their house from Rory's.

"Yes?" Seamus asked.

Rory noted a certain wariness in the question. What did he suspect she wanted to discuss with him?

"Look," she began, "this isn't my business, and I meant to tell you last night..."

He waited.

"I just want to say..." She drew a breath. "Seuss is going to be a large, powerful dog. You've really got to *be* with him, when he's around kids."

"The breeder said they're good with kids."

Rory wanted to kill the breeder. "They can be. But the children have to be considerate. And if there's a lot of running around, squealing, that kind of thing, the dog can get excited. People talk about it arousing their prey drive, but I don't think that's accurate. I mean, a German shepherd is going to realize that your kids aren't prey. But he might still bite. He might think of your kids as puppies and play with them the same way he would with other puppies. I just mean, he needs obedience, and your kids need to be taught what's okay and what's not okay to do around him. And when other kids come over to play, you have to be there to make sure he behaves." She felt her face turn red. This *really* wasn't her business. "I just want things to go right for all of you and Seuss."

Seamus looked at Rory thoughtfully. "I don't suppose *you'd* be willing to teach him obedience."

"It would be better," she said, "for him to go to classes—with you and your kids. He needs to be around other people and other dogs. You've got to make sure he has that experience now, when he's young, so that he's comfortable with these things. I'm sorry for butting in, but…"

"You don't have to apologize. I appreciate what you're saying. Are there classes available in Sultan?"

"I think I might be able to find something. There will probably be just two other dogs, at the most. This is such a small town. But there is a woman who trains avalanche dogs, and she does some obedience classes, too, from time to time. I'd be happy to give you her number."

"Thank you."

His intense study of her made Rory wonder exactly what he was thinking; how he was reacting to her unsolicited advice. She said, "Well, you should grab something to eat, and I'm off to do the same thing. I'll see you at one."

Seamus opened his mouth but didn't speak. Not at once. "Fine," he said at last.

Rory suspected it wasn't what he'd been going to say.

BEAU WAS SULLEN on the ride to the same trail Rory and his father had skied on the previous afternoon. Rory wished she'd been able to speak to him alone about his resistance to telemark skiing—or to skiing with Seamus—but there hadn't been time. Seamus drove, so on the way there Rory sat in the back with Beau and asked him about his previous telemark experience.

"I've done it a few times. I can't, like, make a telemark turn yet."

"Lots of people with tele skis never make a tele turn," Rory replied.

When they reached the spot they'd used the day before, they parked and removed their skis from the roof rack of Seamus's car. As they put on their skis, Rory noticed Seamus watching his son thoughtfully.

"It's been a while since we've skied together, hasn't it?" Seamus asked.

"Yeah," Beau murmured.

"Skins on," Rory said, and they all fitted climbing skins to their skis.

She'd skied with fathers and sons in the past, as a ski instructor. Her pet peeve was fathers who found the occasion an opportunity to pursue her, rather than attend to their children's needs.

Seamus wasn't like that. He complimented Beau, talked about how he himself was huffing and puffing—untrue—while Beau steamed up the trail in the lead. Rory saw Beau's confidence and self-esteem grow with his father's praise. It made her like Seamus more.

In fact, it made her like Seamus to an alarming degree.

Is it just because my father has never spent time with me?

Well, whatever the Lee family got out of the Sultan Mountain School, she reflected, at least they would have this—more time together, meaningful time.

She coached father and son on their first run, praising Beau's form, which was excellent. A childhood skiing in Telluride, even without his father's company, certainly showed.

When they returned to the car late in the afternoon, she checked her cell phone and found a message waiting for her.

"Rory, it's Samantha. We have a domestic problem. Guess who is out and hasn't been found. I've told Desert I'm not sleeping in the house until Lola is caught. So I'll be staying at the hot springs. And Norris broke up with Desert. I think it was about the snake. So Desert's miserable."

And at home alone with Lola? It hadn't been stated in so many words.

Rory certainly wasn't going to sleep in the house with the python loose, either. Granted, Lola was unlikely to cozy up to one of them, bite and squeeze. Still, Rory knew she wouldn't sleep soundly with the snake out of its vivarium.

And Lola would not be easy to catch.

Desert's house, Desert's problem.

But Rory was a roommate. And Desert's boyfriend, according to Samantha, had just broken up with her.

"Everything okay?" Seamus asked as Rory closed the phone.

Rory felt reluctant to reveal that Lola was loose. Desert's irresponsibility—and Rory had no doubt that Desert's carelessness was behind the escape—seemed to reflect on her. *He's going to think we're all like Desert. Airheads*.

Desert *wasn't* an airhead.

She was just…Desert. And though Rory lived with her and danced with her, she had no illusions about the other woman.

Her second thought—after a decision not to tell Seamus about the snake—was that her father mustn't find out.

Anyhow, it wasn't as if Lola would be slithering about in subzero temperatures, menacing the population of Sultan. She was doubtless curled up in some inaccessible part of the house—between the walls, for instance. They might later find her on the move through the house.

Or Desert might have to pay workmen

to come tear apart the place looking for the creature.

"Everything's fine," Rory lied.

Okay, if Desert wanted her to stay in the house, they could sleep in the same room, in case Lola came in and made herself comfortable.

But Rory knew she couldn't get Lola off Desert by herself, and Desert probably couldn't do the same for her. The snake needed three handlers.

Even so, she knew Desert would not abandon the python.

She rode back to the Empire Street house with Seamus and Beau, but she was preoccupied—and unprepared when Beau asked her the plans for the next day.

"I'll drop by this evening, and we can talk about it," she said. "You did really well skiing, Beau."

"What are you doing for dinner?" Seamus asked.

Beau threw a sharp look at his father, then abruptly climbed out of the SUV and started taking his skis off the roof.

"I need to go home and check on something."

"Some evening when Lauren and Beau are willing to babysit, I'd like to take you out to one of the restaurants in town. To thank you for all you're doing for us."

Rory didn't believe the second statement. "I'm just doing my job," she said, with a tone of finality.

He didn't ask again, and she climbed out of the car knowing she'd settled the issue, protected her job and now stood a better chance of pleasing her father.

So why was she disappointed?

She wished that things were different— and that she *was* in a position to enjoy a romantic dinner with Seamus.

CHAPTER FIVE

OVER THE NEXT WEEK, Seamus, Lauren and Beau all completed the avalanche safety course. Beau resumed working for the ski maker, and Rory took Lauren ice-climbing with her. Lauren spent much of her spare time twirling the broom handle Rory had given her. Fiona called and said she'd be ready to join them in Sultan the following week. Seamus assured her that he was enjoying his time with the children.

Fiona asked, "I don't suppose you want to do it all the time, though."

Seamus could tell that, far from trying to influence him—or worse, discourage him from spending time with his family—she was offering him a way out. Perhaps, simply, to see if he would take it.

"Well, when I'm in Telluride it's difficult."

But how true was that?

No, he knew the trouble was that, in the past, he'd felt he needed to avoid the kids.

So far, during the time in Sultan, his children had rarely mentioned Janine.

And yet the issue was there. Always.

He and Fiona hung up with the understanding that she would call him again in a few days to see if he really wanted her to join them. She'd been invited to spend time with her daughter's family, and Seamus sensed she wanted to do it.

ON A THURSDAY evening, more than a week after they'd arrived in Sultan, Lauren arrived home from Rory's fire-dancing class and said to her father, "Rory's like Mom, you know. She can do anything."

Janine *had* been able to do many things. An expert skier, a competent snowboarder, a pilot, an attorney, a mountain biker. Seamus wondered if this would provide him with a chance to talk with Lauren about her mother, to say something that might impress upon Lauren the fact that Janine had still been human. *But how can I explain to her that all her mother's accomplishments may have been signs of her insecurity?* "I don't think

Rory is all that much like your mother," he said instead.

Lauren's expression turned vaguely hostile. "Don't you like Rory?"

"Of course, I like her. I just don't think she's like your mother."

"Why?" Challenging.

Had Lauren somehow worked out the fact that he simply could not speak well of Janine?

He tried, for his daughter's sake. "Your mother was highly educated."

"That doesn't mean anything," Lauren scoffed. "Anyhow, Rory's been to college."

But she hadn't earned a degree, he'd gathered.

He tried to keep his mind on the original subject. "Why do you think she *is* like your mother?"

"She's a really strong person, that's all. A strong woman."

"I agree that Rory is a strong woman."

"And that Mom was."

He said nothing, except, "Let's drop this subject, Lauren."

The teenager glared, and it struck Seamus how much she looked like Janine. His impulse was to phone Fiona at once and tell her to get to Sultan fast. Then he could separate himself from…these feelings. *I'm going to say something. I won't be able to stop myself from saying everything I think about Janine.*

"You were glad Mom died, weren't you?"

The accusation seemed to come out of nowhere. Yet Lauren had pulled it from somewhere within, just as if she *knew* what words would most anger him.

"No," he said. "Please don't say that again."

"You didn't want her to have the gun."

He could not believe that Lauren was bringing this up. "Why is this coming up now?" he asked. "And you're right. I didn't want her to have the gun. It was stupid." The thought came out before he could stop it. But once he'd said it, it seemed especially true. "You were the oldest of our four children."

"She taught me to shoot it."

"What?"

"She wanted me to be strong, like her."

"Your mother *wasn't* strong." There. He'd said it. *Stop, Seamus. Leave—walk away from this. You can't win.* "She spent a whole lot of time trying to prove she was tough. But it didn't make her tough, and it didn't even make her interesting, and it certainly didn't make her any friends." He almost choked as words poured out. "I loved her." The hardest words. "And I was *not* glad she died. Lauren, I *found* her."

Abruptly, his daughter's eyes filled with tears. Throwing her broomstick onto the linoleum like a child half her age, she fled the kitchen. He heard her on the stairs, and then a door slammed. She must have gone into the extra room, the room that would have been hers if she hadn't decided to sleep with Belle.

"Dad?"

He spun. Caleb had come in the back door. How long had he been there? When had he gone outside?

"Where's Seuss?"

"Beau took him. He's watching Rory and her friends dance with fire. I came home."

Seamus considered whether it was safe for a seven-year-old to walk in an alley in Sultan after dark. And whether it was safe for a twelve-year-old to do so.

"Rory lost Lola," Caleb said.

"What?" Seamus couldn't concentrate on what Caleb was saying. He must talk to Lauren. He must find something to say. Now, her mind must be filled with images of what she thought he'd seen when he found Janine.

Nausea coursed through him.

He seldom thought about that discovery anymore. But now the images came flooding back. *Why did I say it? Why did I make her imagine it?*

He'd had counseling after Janine's death—but not recently. The point of counseling had been to talk to another adult, so that he would not talk to his children about what had happened and what he'd seen.

Caleb was saying something, but Seamus didn't listen.

"Caleb, I need to talk to your sister right now. I do want to talk to you, but I need to finish talking with Lauren first. I'll be back."

Upstairs, he knocked on the door of the corner bedroom. "Lauren?"

Feet on the floor. The door swung open. Her beautiful face was tear-streaked.

He said, "Forgive me. Please. I'm so sorry I said those things."

"You meant them," she said.

He couldn't deny it. "I should never have said them to you."

She turned away. "Rory's troupe is going

to perform this weekend for the Sultan Winter Festival."

"We'll have to go see that," he said. He'd been aware of the approaching festival without knowing what it might involve. Relief washed through him. Lauren had changed the subject. They could let it go, move on, pretend they'd never had the conversation. He mused, "I think Caleb said they lost the snake."

"Oh, they did. She's loose in the house somewhere, so Rory and Samantha and Desert are all sleeping in one room. Samantha wasn't going to stay in the house at all, but Desert talked her into it. They're waiting for the snake to turn up. They figure she's curled up next to something warm."

"Undoubtedly." Tension raced through him. Rory was sleeping in that house, living there, with that huge snake wandering around in search of "something warm"? What if it attacked her?

An image came to him of Rory trying to fight off the giant snake. He shook it off, telling himself not to overreact. "Caleb says they're practicing with fire now," he said, to distract them both from thoughts of Lola on the loose.

"I know. You can go watch," she said. "If you want. I mean, I'll stay here with Cal and Belle."

"Thank you. I think I should go see what Beau's up to."

"You want Rory for your next girlfriend, don't you?"

Next girlfriend. As if there'd been a series. As if a girlfriend was a temporary thing, easily replaced by another and another. He gazed at Lauren, noting the arch of her dark eyebrows, her expression belligerent once again.

"Does it matter to you?"

She shrugged. "Someone else is always more important than us. That's all. It's either a girlfriend or work or working out. Then, you say you have no time."

"I've had nothing *but* time since we've gotten to Sultan."

"Beau says you asked Rory out. You can't wait to do something else."

"That's not true."

"I just wish you wanted to be with us, like you obviously want to be with her."

Seamus refused to be drawn in this time.

"I'm going for a walk. Thank you for your generous offer to watch your brother and sister." He looked at her and wanted to say, *I love you, Lauren,* but the words would not come. Not now.

It wasn't that he didn't love her.

But she kept fighting for Janine in the war that was dead, dead, dead.

Except, he knew that it would never be dead. That his children would always cherish their mother's memory—and he never would.

NONE OF THEM were outside. Not Rory and her roommates or their drummer or Beau and Seuss. Was his son inside? With a loose thirteen-foot snake?

Of course, the snake was probably not aggressive....

But look what it did to Samantha. How many stitches had Rory said she'd needed?

He hesitated only a moment. He could see light in the room beyond the back door. He let himself in the back gate and crossed the concrete patio. At the door, he knocked.

He heard laughter, and the door swung open.

It was Rory. She wore a long-sleeved thermal undershirt, baggy canvas pants, a wide-striped knitted scarf and a ski hat. She looked as if she'd just come in from outside, except that she was in her socks.

"Oh, come in. He's here."

Beau knelt on the floor in the carpeted living room. Samantha knelt at the other end of the floor. They seemed to be taking turns saying, "Seuss, come!" and having the puppy rush toward him.

"Dad, he knows 'Come'!" exclaimed Beau.

Where is the snake? Seamus wondered. He said, "Has Lola turned up?"

The tallest roommate, whose hair was now beginning to resemble a buzz cut, wandered in from the hallway. "Oh, hi," she said. She wore flannel pajamas covered with pictures of the Pillsbury Doughboy, and had a red stuffed thing on a ribbon tied around her neck. Seamus saw that it was a heart in two pieces.

"Brokenhearted?" he asked.

She made a face, some sort of agreement.

"Lola is still lost," Rory said, answering his question.

Was that the reason for Desert's heartbreak? He wanted to whisk Rory away from this very odd household. But she wouldn't go. Not while the snake was loose and could hurt her roommates. And part of Seamus found her eccentric lifestyle endearing. She was playful, and so she had found a way to turn her work and her vocations into play.

"Keep Seuss close by," Seamus suggested to his son.

"Seuss would stand up to her, wouldn't you?" Beau asked the puppy.

"Seuss is probably just the right size for a snack for Lola," Seamus answered.

His son suddenly looked as if he might cry. Seamus wished he'd been more tactful, but good grief! Hadn't it occurred to Beau already?

Obviously not, because his son was now hugging the puppy and holding his collar.

"I'm going to take him home," Beau said.

"I'll come with you," Seamus agreed. Was he destined to make all his children cry tonight?

Rory came to Beau's side, bringing the leash, which she fastened onto the puppy's collar and handed to him. "We'll make sure Lola doesn't get him. I'd never let that happen, Beau."

Beau lifted his face with a sort of naked need. A need, perhaps, to be comforted by a babysitter, an older sister, a mother. Rory seemed to fill one of those roles for him.

And she knew just the right thing to say.

"She'll turn up when she gets hungry," Desert said.

Rory wheeled around and looked for a minute as if she was about to yell at her housemate. Then her anger evaporated. She relaxed, breathed.

Was it pointless to address Desert's tactlessness? Seamus supposed so. If Rory were in a serious relationship, would she move out of this house?

"If you're not comfortable sleeping here—any or all of you—we've got plenty of room across the alley," he offered, feeling transparent for doing so. Yes, he wanted Rory under his roof. Rory, who wouldn't even go out to dinner with him.

Desert said, "You don't just *abandon* pets when they get difficult."

"Nobody was suggesting abandoning Lola." Rory managed to sound both reasonable and soothing.

"I've suggested it," Samantha said bluntly.

"I've suggested taking her to the top of Sultan Peak in subzero temperatures and leaving her there."

"She wouldn't live, would she?" asked Beau, seeming puzzled.

"That's the point," Samantha said.

"Let's head home," Seamus suggested. "Rory, we'll be seeing you in the morning?"

She nodded. "Night, Beau. Night, Seuss." She crouched to pet the puppy, who licked her face.

As the door closed behind the Lees, Desert started in on Samantha. "Look, you don't *have* to live here, Samantha. Lola's a member of the family, and it's not nice to talk about killing her."

"It's not nice for her to *try* to kill me, either."

Rory was tired of peacemaking. Lola should never have gotten out. "Rocky Mountain Reptile Rescue has said they'll take her, if we can transport her there."

"Where are they?" asked Samantha at once.

"How are we supposed to contain her to transport her, in the winter, no less?" Desert demanded. "I can't believe you guys are just deciding this on your own. This is *my* house and she's *my* snake."

"Fine." Abruptly, Samantha rose. "I'll move my belongings out tomorrow. I've had enough, Desert. You're my friend, and I love you, but I'm tired of living with that creature wandering the house. I get in the shower and keep peering around the curtain to make sure she hasn't decided to join me in the bathroom. It's not cool. It's not fun. It's scary. Now, we've found a responsible way to solve the problem and you're not willing. You prefer Lola to us. You can keep her."

Exhaustion raced through Rory. She remembered many occasions in years past when *she'd* been the one recovering from a breakup, fired from her job or, most recently, dealing with the loss of a beloved pet. Desert *had* been there for her. Desert could be eminently reasonable. But Lola didn't bring out her better side. Neither had being dumped by Jay Norris.

Yet now, Rory saw the disintegration of their dance troupe—not to mention the friendship between Samantha and Desert. All because of a Burmese python. Why had they ever let Desert acquire the snake? But Burmese pythons were cheap to buy—as cheap to buy as they were expensive to maintain. People in warmer parts of the country sometimes released them into the wild when they grew tired of their pets, where they decimated other populations. Indigo snakes, in the Everglades, for instance. Some localities had ordinances forbidding citizens from owning snakes over a particular length. Of course, there was no ordinance like that in Sultan.

Desert said, "Why don't you just go now? Why don't you just go sleep at the hot springs, like you obviously want to?"

The hot springs had a hostel, as well as rooms for rent, few of them occupied this time of year.

"Desert, if she goes, you and I can't stay. We can't deal with Lola alone, if she gets out of hand."

"She's eaten recently. She's not going to do anything."

Rory closed her eyes. *That's not how it works*. Nobody knew what made a python decide to attack and constrict another creature. Sure, Lola wasn't *likely* to do it…

"I'm not going to sleep somewhere else just

because Lola's loose," Desert said. "Forget it. You're being paranoid."

Rory wasn't sure what to do. All right, she and Desert would be safer together than either one of them would be alone.

"Are you evicting me?" Samantha asked, looking close to tears herself.

One thing was certain. Generous as Seamus's invitation had been, there was no way that Rory was going to take refuge in his house. She would go stay at the hot springs with Samantha.

"Yes!" said Desert. "If you're going to act this way about Lola."

Rory said, "I'm going to bed. If you're not coming in soon, please look in, will you?"

"I'm going to bed, too," Desert answered. "Samantha can do what she wants."

They all ended up in Desert's bedroom, as they had for the past few nights, ever since Lola's escape. Rory closed her eyes and wished fervently that Lola would turn up and that they could transport her immediately to Rocky Mountain Reptile Rescue in Denver. And that no one would get bitten or squeezed in the process.

The phone rang, and Desert took it from her bedside table. "Hello? What? *What?*"

The call was for her, and it wasn't about the python. But it changed everything.

SEAMUS HAD NEVER YET had trouble sleeping, not since he'd come to Sultan. Tonight was an exception. He'd come home to find both Caleb and Belle asleep. Lauren lay on her bed reading a novel in the room she shared with Belle. Lauren hadn't mentioned their earlier argument and neither had Seamus.

We'll just forget about it, he told himself.

Yet tonight, he was the one who couldn't forget. Even more, he couldn't forget the images of Janine that had surfaced. He couldn't quiet the recollection of her unending streams of conversation, always peppered with the latest in skier-surfer-snowboarder slang.

And then this totally sick avalanche runs at us... Seamus tried to remember if she'd always been loud and tough-talking. He must have liked that characteristic once—but he couldn't remember ever feeling that way.

She'd been a youngest child, the youngest of five girls. She'd feigned ignorance of everything remotely related to growing up *as* a girl. She'd never worn dresses and she'd always liked sports. She'd never wanted to own a horse; she'd never played with dolls. She had always, by her own admission, preferred male playmates to female.

As a grown woman, she'd devoted herself to teaching other women to defend themselves, physically as well as legally. Martial arts, of course. She'd been a black belt in aikido, and had an utter lack of humility in regard to her skills.

Seamus had known other men in Telluride who'd come very close to saying—to him, no less—that they didn't care for Janine Jensen. He'd understood that certain men felt threatened by her strength and by her take-all-comers attitude.

Likewise, he'd known that there was something very sweet about her underneath it all.

For instance, her thing for teddy bears. She loved teddy bears—as a hobby, she'd sewn them. Not teddy bears with clothes, because the idea of teddy bears with clothes offended her sensibilities. At the same time, she avoided making Halloween costumes for the children; avoided being known as a woman who *could* sew.

Yes. I loved her.

Though how much he'd *liked* her, especially in the last year, especially after she'd bought the handgun, was another question.

Colorado's full of people who have children and own guns, Janine had said. *You keep the ammo in a separate place and you teach the kids firearms safety.*

Not in Seamus's opinion.

His opinion remained unchanged: Having guns and children in the same house was a recipe for tragedy.

And it wasn't as if she was a law-enforcement officer, for instance, and *needed* a gun for work.

He'd asked her in what situation a handgun would help her against the men she believed to be threatening her. He'd asked why a black belt in aikido needed a handgun to defend herself.

Janine had given him answers, but Seamus had known that all her answers were simply rationalizations. She'd wanted a handgun because she'd wanted to be a woman who owned a handgun.

She'd learned to fly a plane, not because

she loved flying, but because she wanted people to know that she *could* fly a plane.

More skills, more dangerous activities, more risks. And not because she loved the activities in themselves. No.

Because she wanted people to know all the things she could do.

What was it Lauren had said? *You wanted her to die? You were glad she died?*

Not true.

What was true was that, though he couldn't have stopped loving Janine, he had also come to despise her. At some point, he'd lost respect for her—and he hated that in himself.

He didn't judge people that way. He didn't look at a person's accomplishments and *lose respect* for the individual. But Janine had become the enemy—the woman who'd brought a gun into his home. He'd begun to see her as unreasonable, then dangerous in her wrongheadedness, and finally pitiable.

None of those feelings had diminished with her death.

Tonight, what he'd avoided for more than three years had happened. One of his children had spoken admiringly of Janine and he'd been unable to stop himself from voicing his true feelings.

It would happen again, if he continued to spend time with them, and his children would grow to hate him for it. Lauren would, anyhow. And probably Beau.

His feelings weren't going to change, they weren't going away, and they hadn't lessened with time.

"IT'S MY MOTHER." Desert looked stricken.

"What?" Samantha and Rory both moved from their sleeping bags and air mattresses to Desert's bed.

"She has Alzheimer's. My father wants me to come back to Florida." To Boca Raton, where she'd grown up. "So that she can stay at home longer. He asked if I would help."

Rory's own reaction shamed her. A stab of jealousy. Desert's father had asked for her.

Kurt Gorenzi hadn't even spoken with Rory since she'd begun working with Seamus Lee's family. He'd nodded to her in passing twice. Two times, and she remembered each occasion. She imagined a phone call from across the country. *Come home. I need you.*

I would give anything, she thought. And

then she was ashamed of herself. Poor Desert. Having to watch her mother's mental condition deteriorate.

"I've told him I'll go. I didn't tell him about Lola. I could take her with me, I suppose."

Samantha's expression said, *Great idea!*

"We have to find her first," Rory pointed out. But she could imagine the problems of taking apart this two-and-a-half-storey house in order to find a python.

"Would you two stay here and keep renting?" Desert asked. "Or maybe I should sell."

"You don't have to decide anything tonight," Rory told her.

"Except how you're going to find Lola," Samantha replied.

An hour later, Rory was still thinking about Desert's call to come home, to return to her father, an Orthodox rabbi, and her mother. The situation would be fraught with complications for her freedom-loving housemate. Tattoos, piercings, a shaved head—how would all of this go down in Boca Raton?

Yet Desert would have her family. Her family *wanted* her.

CHAPTER SIX

"IF LOLA ISN'T FOUND by Monday morning," Desert said, "I'm going to have some construction guys come in and start taking things apart. There can't be too many places warm enough for her to hide." It was Friday evening, just before the start of the Sultan Winter Festival. Caldera's hour-long performance would kick off a week of events. On Tuesday, Desert would leave to drive to Boca Raton, taking Lola with her in a glass vivarium. Lola would ride in the back of Desert's Toyota Land Cruiser. Desert was putting her house on the market. Until it sold, Rory and Samantha would continue to live there.

"You're sure, then," Rory cautioned, "that you'll want to stay in Florida. I mean, what if…" She didn't want to finish her question. What if Desert still didn't get along with her family, as she hadn't growing up?

"If it doesn't work out, I'm going to look

for a place down in the Keys. There are some massage schools there I want to check out, and maybe I'll look into learning acupuncture."

"You're really a free spirit," Samantha murmured.

"You and Rory can keep performing together," Desert pointed out. They were all in the living room of Desert's house, using the big Victorian mirrors, with their ornate gilded frames, as they dressed and did their makeup. Rory and Samantha tied their hair back, severely adorning it with cowrie falls. They would soak their heads before the fire sets. All three young women pressed *bindi,* small false jewels, to their foreheads between their eyebrows in the position of the third eye. They applied eyeliner and dressed themselves with coin bras and heavy silver jewelry. The night's performance would take place inside the Sultan Recreation Center—with firemen standing by.

Rory planned to pick up her grandmother and give her a ride to and from the performance. So when she was dressed, she set out in her car.

Rory loved to perform, loved the almost

hypnotic pleasure of working with blazing poi, and loved the drama of tribal-fusion belly dance. She felt no nerves before these performances.

Now she pulled up outside the two-storey Victorian where she'd grown up. Before she'd even parked, the front door of the house was open. Rory left the engine running while she went up the sweeping concrete steps to the hillside house.

Sondra Nichols stepped out, dressed to the nines, all in white.

"You're beautiful," Rory told her.

"No. I'm old. *You* are beautiful. Your father told me you're doing lovely things at the Sultan Mountain School."

Rory's heart soared. "He did?"

"Yes. I think his client's very impressed by your way with his children."

In spite of herself, Rory rolled her eyes. "The *client* should spend some time with those children."

Sondra glanced at her once. "He doesn't?"

"For a while, he seemed to want to be with them. But he has obviously recovered from that impulse. He's not quite as bad with the younger two, but he treats the older ones like they have the plague." *A bit like my father has always treated me,* she thought grimly. Something she and her grandmother had discussed through the years. "And, of course, they *long* for his attention."

As if reading her mind, Sondra said, "I can imagine that wouldn't win him any points with you. Any idea what the trouble is?"

"Not really. I assume he prefers grown-ups."

"Do you think that's how *your* father felt, Rory?"

"I think my father is angry at my mother— or at least he was when I was growing up. I think he didn't want anything to do with me because of it."

Sondra Nichols neither confirmed nor challenged this picture. In the car, she fastened her seat belt. "You look very like her, you know."

Rory lifted her eyebrows. "Not from any photograph I've seen."

"It's subtle. It's in your expressions and the way you laugh."

They arrived at the recreation center, where their drummers were carrying equipment inside. Three men would be providing live drumming for part of their performance.

As Rory lugged her heaviest tote bag, she spotted Lauren and Beau approaching the rec center.

They waved, and Rory waited at the deck railing for them to reach her. Her grandmother lingered beside her, intrigued by the children.

"Can we watch you set up?" Lauren asked. "Hi, Mrs. Nichols," she added.

Rory was impressed. It was a week since Lauren had met her grandmother.

"Hello, Lauren. It's nice to see you again."

"Of course, you can watch." Normally, Rory would have discouraged other people hanging around while the troupe set up, but she liked these children. Maybe it was that she, like they, knew what it was to wish for a father's love and attention. Maybe it was that she, like they, had no mother. Maybe it was that she kept wanting to *help* Lauren— Lauren, who was so impressed with her dead mother, who clearly missed her and wanted to be like her.

Though Rory had grown up motherless, she'd never felt a desire to be *like* her mother.

Sometimes like her grandmother, yes, because her grandmother had such a love of life. But part of what troubled her about Lauren—*and* made her protective toward the girl—was her own certainty that the picture Lauren had of her mother was inaccurate. Rory's own picture of the person described by Samantha and Seamus, as well as by Lauren and Beau, felt incomplete. Yet a part of that picture was of a type of woman—sort of brash, making "strength" a virtue, while true strength wasn't necessarily the quality demonstrated. More like bravado.

Of course, she could be wrong.

She gave Beau the job of carrying the prepared fire staffs into the rec center. "Are Belle and Caleb going to be able to come and watch?" Rory asked.

"Fiona's bringing them," Beau said, sounding unenthusiastic.

Rory's stomach dipped. Who was Fiona?

A girlfriend of Seamus's, no doubt.

Which shouldn't bother her at all. In fact, it should bother her so little that she definitely wouldn't ask if Seamus himself would be coming to watch the performance.

Lauren's expression mirrored her brother's.

While Samantha cued a CD and Desert talked to the drummers and the firemen, double-checking safety procedures related to the fire performance, Rory watched her grandmother with Seamus's two oldest children, both of whom seemed to enjoy talking with her. She was proud of Sondra, proud of the woman she was. Though she was older now, she remained attractive and fit and entirely capable of relating to teenagers. Never, in all Rory's years of growing up with Sondra, had her grandmother *embarrassed* her.

Fiona, Rory decided, would be blond and gorgeous and expensively dressed—very Telluride. Undoubtedly, she'd be staying in Sultan with Seamus's family for the remainder of their stay here. *Another excuse for him to ignore his own kids,* Rory thought bitterly.

Her father would be here tonight, but she didn't kid herself that he would be coming to see her perform. This was a community event and he would be here to promote the interests of the town.

All the pleasure and excitement she'd felt earlier had begun to fade. She didn't have to think about why, didn't want to think about why.

Fiona.

Fiona, who would be bringing Caleb and Belle.

Seamus might not even bother to come, and if he came she might feel worse. Seeing him with Fiona.

"Are you all right?" Samantha asked, as the three dancers waited in the kitchen of the community center.

Rory nodded, checking again to make sure that her hair and Samantha's was completely soaked with water and that no stray tendrils were hanging loose.

Samantha cast her a penetrating look. "You like him, don't you?"

"Who?" Rory asked.

Samantha smirked slightly, then turned away. Abruptly, she swung back. "I think he's probably a pretty decent guy, Rory. Reading between the lines of the story Janine mapped out."

"It doesn't *matter,*" Rory hissed at her. "I just wish he liked spending time with his kids. And you didn't hear me say that." Then, she softened her tone. "But thank you for asking. Thanks for everything." Impulsively, she hugged her friend.

Then, they heard the director of the local public radio station welcoming everyone to the festival. At this cue, they filed out into the hall carrying their fire staffs, and their drummer, Woody, lit the wicks, setting the staffs ablaze. The lights had been turned off, and now the fire staffs and glowing exit signs provided the only light in the room.

Rory no longer thought of Seamus Lee. There was no room for anything but the task at hand. Fire-dancing required complete concentration, and Caldera's combinations of movement demanded perfect execution.

The first number went flawlessly.

While they doused the wicks in the back corridor and exchanged their staffs for poi, the percussionists beat a fast tattoo. The women filed back out, poi swinging in perfect time.

Rory began to feel the sheer pleasure of the performance. This sort of art, for her, was not about showing others what she could do, as much as it was the joy of working in sync with the other two dancers. Sometimes it seemed as if a tide connected them; as if her arms were guided by a force that also guided Desert's and Samantha's, so that all of them moved in perfect harmony.

This show marked the last time—at least the last time for a while—that Caldera would perform as a group.

But Rory couldn't and didn't think of this, either. She gave herself up to the fun of spinning poi.

When their fire-dancing segments were over, the applause was thunderous. Most of the audience was standing, anyhow, to watch, although some, including Rory's grandmother, sat at tables along the walls and windows. Rory could see no one in the dark as she left the stage. The dancers doused the poi balls, and Rory and Samantha hurried to let down their hair.

When they returned to the stage, lights had been turned on and Rory saw Seamus. He stood against one wall beside her father, and both men had their eyes on the stage.

Rory allowed herself a small smile of greeting—to her father—and quickly looked for Caleb and Belle. She might as well see what Fiona looked like. But Caleb and Belle sat at a table on the opposite side of the room from Seamus. With them was an elderly woman with long gray-and-white hair in a single braid. She wore a flannel shirt and jeans and looked like a mountain woman.

So, Fiona was *not* a girlfriend.

But *why* wasn't Seamus with his kids?

Lauren stood in the back of the room talking to the lift operator from the Sultan ski area. Bobby Briggs was about twenty-two, Rory thought. He'd served in the military and then returned to Sultan, where he'd grown up. He was very handsome, with the bones of a *GQ* model, and she was unsurprised that Lauren had been keen to talk with him.

Bobby was no fool. He wasn't going to mess around with a girl Lauren's age—supposing he'd wanted to, which was unlikely. But he did enjoy having a harem of admirers at the ski slope.

Where was Beau?

By himself. Standing near the windows with a black expression.

Oh, Seamus.

It was the last thought Rory could afford to give any of them. At the moment, she needed to focus on Desert. Rory echoed her friend's movements, following through backward figure eights, taxim and clock floreos, and then Samantha followed Rory's movements, and again Rory became connected to the tide of movement, in rhythm with her partners. Goddess arms behind veils, then the twirling aside of veils, a giant pinwheel of silk.

She would not look at Seamus Lee again.

"DOES IT BOTHER YOU, seeing your daughter doing that?" Seamus asked Kurt Gorenzi during a break.

Kurt's stern expression didn't change. "Which part?"

"Any of it. The fire. The costumes. Sensual dance."

"It's belly dance, not stripping," Kurt answered tersely. "It's an ancient art form and Rory says it's a celebration of femininity. It's people with their minds on one thing, who insist on interpreting it as something different. Rory and her friends are professional dancers." He was silent. "Anyhow, I've not exactly set myself up to have a say in what she does with her life."

"Do you regret that?"

Kurt slid his eyes sideways to look at Seamus but didn't answer.

The music turned fast, and Seamus stood

spellbound at the skill of the dancers, who could isolate each muscle, each bone. They were beautiful, all of them, and their skill at this tempo left him feeling like an idiot for suggesting to Kurt Gorenzi that the other man *ought* to have a problem with his daughter's appearing on stage in a coin bra and flared black pants, her hair trailing beads and feathers and cowrie shells.

Seamus knew he was in trouble. It had happened without his awareness. He was captivated by Rory Gorenzi, spellbound and enchanted. He thought about her dozens of times every day.

His feelings were involved to an extent he'd not have believed possible. He couldn't remember *ever* feeling this way about a woman.

Quite simply, he was *certain* that he wanted her to be a permanent part of his life, a permanent part of his children's days and nights. He had found someone precious and already he knew that he didn't want to lose her.

Yet she wasn't his to lose, and she showed no sign of becoming so. In the past several days, she'd become more aloof, though she treated his kids as thoughtfully as ever. The fact that she cared about them couldn't be plainer.

Nor could the fact that she had no time for him.

When Caldera's performance ended, he wandered back into the lobby, to make sure she didn't leave before he'd had a chance to speak with her.

"Dad!"

It was a strangely unfamiliar cry, and he turned to see Caleb running through the corridor toward him.

"Are you leaving?" Caleb said. "I want to ride with you."

"Fiona has the car keys. I walked."

"Then, can I walk with you?"

"Not now. I want to talk to Rory."

Something slipped over his son's face, a mask that said Caleb understood nothing, except that he was being brushed off by his father. That his father didn't want his company.

Seamus felt the rejection bounce back and strike him, as if he somehow felt the same pain Caleb had just experienced. Yet he couldn't speak, didn't know what to say.

"Where's Fiona?" Seamus managed to ask his son.

Caleb said, "In there. Are you coming back in?"

"I don't know. I'll see you at home." He turned, then, and saw her. She'd emerged from the kitchen with two carryalls, in the pants she'd worn for her performance, her parka covering her top. Her hair was still adorned with feathers and shells, and she was wearing snow boots and her down jacket. "Rory."

But she was already hugging Caleb.

"You have to meet Fiona!" Caleb said.

"I want to very much. Can I do that tomorrow, Caleb?"

"Okay," Caleb said happily, in contrast to the way he'd reacted to Seamus not walking home with him.

As Caleb ran back to the room where the others waited, Seamus gestured toward Rory's burdens. "May I help you carry things out to your car?"

She seemed to consider briefly. "Yes."

He relieved her of the heavier tote bag and held open the door, to let her lead the way. She started the car and let it idle while she loaded it.

"Your troupe is amazing," Seamus said.

"You were great—I had no idea, even after seeing you practice."

"Thank you."

She closed the back door. "Well, that's everything. Thanks. I need to get home and get some sleep."

"I heard Desert's moving away."

"Yes. Her father needs her help."

"It surprises me that she's going. She doesn't seem…"

"People often aren't what they seem." Rory cut him off.

"Rory, do we have a problem? You seem—a bit cool lately."

He noted that she didn't answer at once, that she seemed to be thinking over how to respond.

But actually, Rory was trying to *keep* from responding. Trying to *keep* from saying exactly what she thought. Partly this was prompted by the suspicion that she wanted to talk with him because she was attracted to him; because she couldn't keep from thinking about him. She felt vulnerable, afraid of her own impulses. If she began telling Seamus what she thought…

If only she could keep her own counsel, for once.

Her grandmother had opted to ride home with her friend Malcolm, the town judge, and Rory longed to get home and take a hot shower. She wished she could drop into bed without worrying about the still-missing python. Tonight, she was going to take her chances, in any case. "Actually," she said, "I'm downright cold. Desert said it's five below right now. And I don't think it's going to get warmer tonight." She climbed into the driver's seat of her car.

"Why don't you run me home with you and we'll talk on the way?"

"Get in," she said, wondering how she was going to stay out of trouble in this conversation.

Seamus walked around the vehicle and slid into the passenger seat.

As they fastened their seat belts, Rory said, "Your children want your attention. That's all. If I sound cool, that's probably what it's about. You have a great family. I really like your kids."

"They like you."

Rory looked at him, perplexed. Did he simply *not care* about his children? She hadn't believed that earlier. Maybe she hadn't wanted to believe it. She said, "Look, it's a little personal for me. My own father has never exactly been an integral part of my life. And I never had a chance to know my mother—she died when I was little. I know her only from the picture my grandmother paints of her. I feel for your kids, because I know what it is to want the attention of the only parent you have."

Seamus understood.

And maybe she thought he was more interested in chasing her than in taking care of his kids, than in giving them the love they needed.

But how could he explain the facts?

He couldn't. He didn't want to talk about Janine to anyone.

He didn't want to speak of her death. There was no way to describe the experience of finding his wife like that; the terror of what might have happened if one of the children had found her instead, had seen what he'd seen, had picked up the handgun. Just out of curiosity. Beau, for instance, at nine, fascinated by all things, wanting to know how everything worked. Or Caleb, who had been four.

And Rory, sensible woman that she was, would probably suggest he get some therapy. But he'd *had* therapy.

Therapy was not going to make him less angry at Janine.

Therapy was not going to make *any* of it better.

What made it better—or had seemed to make it bearable until he'd come to Sultan— was avoidance. Avoiding his children, and especially any instance in which he might tell them his real opinion of their mother, his recollections of her death, any of it, all of it.

"I love my children," he finally said. "I'm…angry about the way Janine died. I'd prefer not to share that anger with them."

Oh.

Rory considered this. Couldn't he spend time with his kids without Janine's death coming into it?

Maybe not. Maybe that would be difficult to avoid, indeed. Because it wasn't necessarily the kind of thing people were *supposed* to avoid.

"I lost it with Lauren last week," he admitted. "I said too much."

"That must be difficult to keep from doing," Rory reflected. "I have that problem in everyday life—without big issues at stake." And Lauren, Rory reflected, considered her mother to be a heroine. A role model.

It was possible that Seamus actually hated Janine. For buying a gun and then dying because of it.

"Wow," she said, as much to herself as to him. "This seems like a big issue. Really big. But Seamus, your kids need you." The answer came to her even as she spoke. "They need to be with you more than they need *not* to see you angry with their mother. Maybe they'll be mad at you for not loving her or supporting her memory the way they think you should. But they'll be more angry—or something worse than angry—if you avoid them, rather than lose your temper in front of them.

"It's kind of like my situation, I think. My mom was being unfaithful to my dad when she died, and I think that's part of why he's never had much to do with me. It's not... adult...to act that way." One of her hands flew from the steering wheel to cover her mouth. Had she really said that about her father? Had she said that his reaction to her mother's death—his treatment of her, his daughter—was immature? "I didn't mean that. I don't know what I mean. These aren't easy things."

But Seamus was thinking about what she said. "You think I should just risk it."

"Well, you've *got* to talk to other adults, someone, about how you feel. Then, maybe you won't need to talk to your kids about it. I mean, if I were a parent and my spouse bought a handgun, I would be frightened. I would be mad at him for making a unilateral decision. I think lots of people would probably feel the way you do. Have you ever talked to anyone about that?"

"You mean a counselor? Yes. For quite some time. But I'm still angry, and I'm still not willing to go through the motions with my children, pretending that I think their mom was a great person. She was insecure and stubborn and seemed to have a native inability to *listen.* It makes me sick that Lauren sees her as the patron saint of all things wise and strong."

It was the first time Rory had heard venom in his voice. They'd reached his house, and now she slowed in front.

"Wouldn't you like me to help you carry everything into your house?" he asked.

"I can manage."

"Did you find the python?"

"Actually, no."

"So it's not really safe for you to be there alone."

Rory shook her head. "Don't worry about it. The chance of Lola reappearing and getting aggressive with me is slight."

"But such things *do* happen," he pointed out.

"I wish she would turn up," Rory admitted. "Look, I have your number. I'll call if there's a problem. Samantha and Desert will be home in a few hours."

Seamus reluctantly headed up the walk, just as his SUV pulled up to the curb behind Rory's car. Fiona was back with the children.

Rory drove away, her mind on Seamus, on her initial prejudice against him, and on what really lay beneath his distance from his children. The problem was not what she'd imagined. She respected his wish not to criticize Janine in front of his children, but in his voice this evening she'd heard something close to hatred. His fear did not seem unreasonable to her. His feelings on the subject were neither mutable nor casual.

She let herself in the back door of the pink house and switched on the mudroom light, then carried her gear inside and looked around.

Lola was curled on top of the refrigerator.

"Lola!" Rory said happily. "You're back." Remembering her promise to Seamus, she dialed the number of the Empire Street house.

The voice of an elderly woman answered. "Hello?"

"This is Rory Gorenzi," she said, watching Lola stir slightly, looking toward her. "Is Seamus there?"

"Yes."

A moment passed, and Seamus picked up the phone. "Rory?"

She told him about Lola. "I'll watch to make sure we don't lose her again, but it's rather difficult to carry her without three people. It's warm up there, and she looks as though she wants to stay where she is, actually."

"But I don't think you should be alone with her," Seamus put in. "Do you?"

"It would be extremely unusual if anything happened," Rory reassured him. No, the situation wasn't ideal, but it could be remedied when her roommates came home. "I'll call Desert on her cell phone right now."

"Yes," he said. "I'll see you soon." He hung up.

Desert didn't answer her phone. Rory had just finished leaving her a message when a knock sounded at the back door. She opened it and Seamus came in—he was so tall and sober and seemed so competent. Something warm and unnerving rushed through Rory.

"Your father's coming, too," he said. "So we can move her."

"She doesn't actually weigh that much," Rory said. "I was thinking of when there are three women. That's how many we need to move her in case she gets, you know, restive."

A moment later she heard a knock at her front door and hurried to answer it. Her father stood there. "Um. Hi," she said. "This really wasn't necessary."

"I was seized with a desire to see the great

Burmese python before it moves away," he told her.

Yes. The grapevine. No secrets in Sultan.

Without comment, Rory led him through the living room with its antique furnishings, which Desert intended to sell with the house, and past the ornate staircase with its Victorian moldings. He admired the iron stove in the hall and the decorative radiator. "Lovely place," he said as they stepped into the kitchen and he saw the patterned linoleum that Desert had so carefully uncovered. "I'm astonished she's selling."

"Actually, she's begun to fantasize about antebellum mansions in the south. Though I don't think she'll have much time on her hands for a while."

"Ah," said her father, glancing up and spotting Lola, peacefully sleeping.

"Well," said Rory. "Let me go downstairs and make sure her water dish is full and everything."

"Fine." He turned to Seamus, and together the men admired the kitchen light fixtures. "This is a showplace," Kurt said. "She's asking half a million, and the market will bear it. I had no idea it was like this inside."

Her father. Her father had come to help her. What conclusions he was drawing about a woman who needed help because of an escaped Burmese python was another question. She'd spent most of her life assuming that her father disapproved of her. But now that she was actually working for him—well, he didn't treat her as though he disapproved of her. He was simply aloof.

Was *he* angry with her mother for dying?

He must have been angry with her for betraying him with another man. Rory had always known that. But she'd assumed that he extended that anger, unfairly, to her. What if he, like Seamus, feared speaking ill of her mother in front of her? What if he was protecting her from his anger toward her mother, just as Seamus tried to protect his children?

"THAT'S A BIG SNAKE," Kurt remarked to Seamus while Rory was downstairs.

"Too big," Seamus agreed. "It belongs in a zoo, not in a house."

Kurt made no answer.

Seamus said, "You must be proud of Rory." He was fishing, fishing because of the conversation he'd had with Rory in her car. Her frank admission of how his children wanted his company and her sense of rejection by her father. He wanted to hear Kurt Gorenzi say that he *did* care about his daughter, that he thought she'd matured into a fine human being.

Kurt simply looked at him. Then, he said, "Why?"

Seamus could not believe his ears. "She can do so many things." *Don't bluster, Seamus.* "She has an amazing degree of knowledge of the backcountry. She's *great* with children."

"You've said that. She is a remarkable human being, but I can't claim to have had much to do with it."

That was better. Maybe that was regret in Kurt's voice. No, it was simply acceptance of the status quo, of the reality he'd created.

But slowly, another possibility occurred to Seamus. *He knows you'd like to sleep with his daughter.* Of course Kurt wasn't going to go overboard in his enthusiasm for the subject of his daughter's merits. Seamus sincerely doubted that Rory was a virgin, but maybe Kurt found that having a friend who was little more than a decade younger than himself pursue Rory was too close for comfort.

Well, too bad, Seamus thought. Understanding the reason behind Rory's coolness toward him had given him room for hope.

He glanced around the interior of the Victorian house with a new thought in mind.

Desert was selling it.

Furnished.

Of course, his kids still had ties to Telluride.

But Rory had made him believe that what they wanted most of all was the love and attention of their father.

She emerged at the top of the basement steps. "Well, let's do it," she said matter-of-factly and drew one of the kitchen chairs over to the refrigerator and stood up. She stroked the sleeping snake. "Lola, wake up."

"They're deaf," her father said.

"But they feel vibrations, and I think she might know the vibration of my voice. She has certainly encountered my scent before."

It was a simple and painless operation, Rory taking Lola's head, Seamus her middle and Kurt the tail.

"This is really overkill," Rory told them

on the way down the stairs. "Two of us could have done it easily."

"Or one," Kurt said.

"Yes, but that's not a good idea—at least not without someone else around. They're very strong. Snakes."

"What would an animal like this kill in the wild?" Kurt asked.

"I'm not sure. Lola eats frozen rabbits, as you know." Because of the rabbits in the freezer at the Sultan Mountain School. Her feelings about Desert's departure were mixed. Rory would miss her friendship, miss dancing with her, miss her sense of humor. She would not miss Lola, or Desert's annoying habit of assuming that other people should understand why she did all the things she did.

Rory was envious of her housemate's situation—no money worries, because of her wealth, *and* she was being invited back into her family. She was *needed* by her family. Also, Rory suspected that the experience of caring for her mother as her Alzheimer's progressed would somehow *help* Desert, steady her, give her a sense of purpose and greater self-confidence, the kind of true confidence that comes from knowing one is useful, valuable. Needed.

She secured the door of the vivarium, leaving the Burmese python inside.

"She's an impressive creature," Kurt remarked, gazing through the glass at the snake. "I think I can see why your roommate's reluctant to part with her."

Rory made no answer. She doubted her father actually did see why. Desert *loved* Lola as one loved a pet. Finally, she said, "They can grow to twenty feet and two hundred pounds."

"Wow!" exclaimed Kurt.

"Yes," Seamus echoed. "My son Beau was quite worried about this one possibly eating our puppy. That was my fault. For mentioning the chance."

Kurt smiled ruefully. He scanned the floor, as though looking for something, then eyed his daughter, and his expression was a bit troubled. "Will you get another dog?" he finally asked.

She was touched. She'd never mentioned Gandalf's death to him, and yet he knew. "I don't know. Desert is the one who was allergic. But I may not be able to stay in this house after it sells, and a dog needs a fenced yard."

Seamus said, "Could we see… Maybe it's not a good time." After all, Rory hadn't washed off her makeup or even so much as taken off her down jacket. "I'd love to see the whole house. Since it's on the market."

Kurt nodded. "So would I. Perhaps another day? Or maybe you'll have an open house for prospective buyers."

"Yes. Maybe," said Rory, with sadness.

CHAPTER SEVEN

DESERT DROVE AWAY from the house on the following Tuesday, with Lola carefully contained in her portable vivarium in the back of Desert's Land Cruiser. She also pulled a U-Haul trailer, but she'd chosen to give many of her possessions to her friends upon departing. She'd given Rory several of her favorite hip belts for belly dancing and Samantha a metal cone bra made for her in New York. There were also earrings, rings from Africa, Bedouin bracelets, and many other personal belongings that had somehow been part of their life with Caldera.

"We'll choose a new name," Samantha had promised. "Because even if we can find another dancer or more dancers, the troupe won't be the same without you."

Minutes after Desert had left, Samantha and Rory decided on the name Turquoise

Sky, a tribute to the fall sky over Colorado's mountains.

The Realtor Desert had chosen loved the idea of an open house and chose Valentine's Day as the date. If the house hadn't sold by summer, they could host another one then.

All that was required of Rory and Samantha was to keep their own rooms clean. The Realtor's crew took care of the rest, cleaning furnishings and floors, carpets and upholstery and polishing the antiques. On the morning of Valentine's Day they would bring in flowers, food and wine.

Seamus's family was a month into its course with the Sultan Mountain School. Beau had been promoted from intern to wage earner at the ski factory, and Lauren was teaching the tiny tots snowboard class every morning at eleven. Caleb was participating in junior avalanche school and competing in local snowboarding competitions. All the children had academic classes in the afternoon, now, with Sultan Mountain School teachers. Essays, creative writing, artwork and more were part of the program.

Rory noticed that with Fiona Murray on the premises, she saw less of the Lee children but more of Seamus. Fiona, clearly, made it possible for Seamus to distance himself from his children.

Seamus had taken to stopping by in the evenings, sometimes bringing her a cup of chai tea from the neighborhood coffee stand, sometimes just to tell her of something he'd seen in Sultan or something he wanted her to see. Or he'd use the excuse of the puppy, Seuss, whom Beau was taking to obedience classes at the Sultan Recreation Center once a week. There were only two dogs in the class, plus the instructor's demonstration dog.

Seamus would always invite Rory to come for a walk with him in the evening. And Rory would always refuse, even as she felt herself being drawn to him in every way. The physical attraction was so overwhelming that she longed to ignore professionalism and let the relationship go wherever it would.

Finally, one evening when he'd invited her for a walk as usual, she tried to explain. "You're a Sultan Mountain School client and I'm an SMS employee. It's not…on. You know what I mean."

He'd nodded thoughtfully and had stopped

inviting her for walks, but he continued to approach her in friendship.

Rory told herself that he wouldn't *always* be a client.

But when he was no longer a client, he and his family would return to Telluride, unless her father's plans came to pass. She knew that Kurt would like nothing better than for Seamus, his family, his studio and his employees all to move to Sultan.

On Valentine's Day, Rory worked as usual. She and Seamus went up to nearby Robin Mountain to telemark ski. They reviewed avalanche skills on the way, taking time to dig a pit that would indicate avalanche conditions in the area. Concluding that conditions were sufficiently safe, they skied for two hours. Rory realized while they were skiing that she had come to know his scent. Sometimes, he touched her, casually, appropriately, on the shoulder or back, to get her attention.

At home after skiing that day, Rory quickly showered and then dressed in black wool slacks and jacket with a white blouse. Samantha wore a batik dress with a metal belt. The Realtor and caterers were in place before five, when visitors began to arrive.

Carpenters had done a bit of work on some of the upstairs rooms and the house looked lovely. Old, but largely restored.

Seamus and his children arrived without Fiona. Rory asked after her, and Seamus said, "She actually left today to visit her daughter and grandchildren."

Rory darted a look at him. "And you're comfortable with that?"

He flipped a hand, indicating ambivalence.

Lauren came over to join them. "What is going to happen to your troupe without your friend?"

"Samantha and I will perform without her. We've changed the name. If we find new troupe members, we'll add them. But we have a functioning duo in the meantime."

"I wish I was good enough," Lauren said.

"You will be. You have a natural gift for dance," Rory told her. "I think you can do just about anything you want, Lauren."

Seamus's older daughter beamed. "If we lived here," she said, "I'd want to work really hard at my dancing and staff spinning until I could be in your troupe."

Rory envisioned this for a moment, and knew that she was really envisioning something more, some closer tie between her and this girl. *If I had a sister,* she thought, *I'd like her to be like Lauren.*

Of course, if she and Seamus…

"Would you like to live here?" Seamus abruptly asked Lauren.

"Yes," answered Lauren, so swiftly that Rory wondered if there was something going on in the girl's life in Sultan that none of them knew about. Yes, Lauren liked to flirt with Bobby, the lift operator. And there were some other young guys around, as well.

But Lauren was only fourteen.

Suddenly, Rory felt certain that a boy was behind Lauren's desire to live in Sultan. And this made her uneasy. Because Sultan boys of Lauren's age were usually in school during the day. And Rory herself didn't know all the kids in town.

The downside of Sultan's economic re-awakening was the number of new people in town. Many college-aged boys came to learn avalanche science, work for the ski areas in the mountains and simply bum around and ski the backcountry.

Somebody better find out what that girl's up to, she thought.

Seamus asked Rory, "Can I get you a glass of wine?"

"Sure… Thanks. Red."

She saw her father come through the front door. She nodded to him. He had some people with him whom she didn't recognize—perhaps these were more strangers he was helping to sell on the idea of Sultan as a place to live. Maybe investors.

Lauren wandered off. She was wearing expensive-looking Telluride clothes, hip-hugger jeans and a tight-fitting top that accentuated her figure. *She could pass easily for older than fourteen,* Rory thought.

As Seamus handed her a glass of wine, Rory said, "I wonder if Lauren has a boyfriend we don't know about."

"She's dating someone I know about," Seamus answered. "His name's Silas. He's new to the area, homeschooled, I think."

"You've met him."

"You're worrying me," Seamus remarked. "Yes, I met him. I haven't met his parents, I'll admit, but he's come by the house twice to pick up Lauren. She comes home on time."

Rory did not understand why she felt so

suspicious of a boy she'd never met. But it was there, and it was her intuition.

She paid attention to her intuition. It told her when to avoid particular slopes, even if it looked like there was no danger of avalanche; when *not* to take that last run of the day. It had told her that Gandalf's final illness was serious and would take him from her.

Too much to hope it was wrong now.

"You might...check up on things," Rory said. "I don't know anyone by that name, but you're new in town, as well. It's not as though you've lived here for years and know everyone."

"Did you date when you were fourteen?"

"I never dated until college, Seamus."

"Where did you go to school?"

"It was just one year. At Fort Lewis, in Durango. School wasn't really... I tend to like jobs that I learn from experience. I've never been that successful in the classroom."

"Why didn't you date before college?"

She laughed. "I grew up here. Your schoolmates here are more like family. The biggest number of kids I ever had in my class was five."

"Wow," Seamus remarked. "Is it that way still?"

"It's changing. There are lots of little kids now. But last year's high school graduating class only had seven students."

He looked alarmed, perhaps realizing how different the educational process would be for his children if they moved to Sultan.

He saw Lauren across the room, talking to a woman who looked as if she might be in college. As one, they laughed at some joke, both doubling over. Rory followed his gaze.

"Who's that?" he said.

"I don't know her name. She's a barista at the coffeehouse. You know, she makes lattes and stuff."

His lips twitched. "I know what a barista is. I just wondered how Lauren knew her."

"I think she goes in there for coffee sometimes before teaching skiing lessons," Rory said. "She said you let her drink coffee."

"I do. I probably shouldn't."

Rory shrugged. "I'd be the wrong person to ask about this. I love the stuff. I don't know if it's worse for teenagers than it is for anyone else."

The Realtor spotted Seamus. "There you

are," she exclaimed, stepping over and taking his arm. "We were just about to tour the second floor. Please join us."

Rory noticed that her father's entourage was waiting for the tour, as well. She said she'd remain downstairs, to give the others more room. In fact, she wanted to join Lauren and her barista friend and do some detective work regarding Silas. But before she could move in that direction, her father joined her.

"I'm going to wait," he said. "Let them go up themselves. After all, I'm not in the market for a big Victorian."

Rory nodded. She hoped that he thought she looked professional. She'd wanted to look refined for the open house, although the event had little to do with her or Samantha.

"I wanted to let you know..." Her father seemed to hesitate.

Rory glanced at him.

"You seem to be keeping Seamus within appropriate bounds. That's what I expect from employees."

Offended—even as she thought about her many impulses to yield to Seamus's various invitations—Rory said, "It goes without saying."

"Then I apologize for saying it. He's taken with you. He's wealthy, ambitious, a nice guy for all that, and I hope he moves here. But entanglements tend to produce a different result."

Rory blinked once and thought of telling him that the question was moot, she wasn't interested. But that would be a lie. Instead, she took umbrage at the word *entanglements*. She knew she should let it be. But *he* wasn't a client. He was her employer, yes, but good grief, he'd brought this up.

"You think he's interested in an 'entanglement'?" she finally asked. "A casual fling?"

He took a quick breath, opened and shut his mouth. "I think even the best of intentions can lead to entanglements."

"You think a man couldn't have serious feelings for me?" She couldn't stop because he *was* her father.

"Probably not that one," Kurt answered bluntly.

The back of Rory's eyes grew hot. With horror, she feared she was going to cry. Not because of anything to do with Seamus. But because her own father thought Seamus Lee was too good for her. *I can't say anything. Nothing is the only thing to say.*

"You just don't have much in common," he shrugged. "You're an extremely competent outdoorswoman, but he's an entrepreneur, an artist, a world traveler. He's back and forth between here and Japan. I think for a long-term commitment he's unlikely to pick someone who has spent her whole life in Sultan, Colorado."

You jerk, was all she could think.

"You've spent your life here," she said.

"Yes. But your mother had a much broader experience, and it created some conflict. She was a world traveler, studying plants on nearly every continent."

Rory was afraid to say more or ask more. It was the first time her father had ever even come close to discussing his relationship with her mother. Was he implying that because he and her mother had come from different backgrounds, that had somehow led to her mother's infidelity?

She said, softly, "I'm sorry she was unfaithful. But it was never my fault."

Her father didn't answer at once. He stared thoughtfully at one of the antiques, a marble-topped highboy across the room. "She felt tied down by having a child. She did like to travel, yet she was also determined to keep nursing you. She used to leave you with your grandmother and go skiing. Every day. For hours. I thought she was just skiing." His look was rueful. "You're right. It wasn't your fault."

But Rory understood what he believed. It lay beneath his words. It hadn't been her fault. And yet it had.

He said, "It was hers."

Everything inside her shifted again, and it was like hearing Seamus speak about Janine. *It was her fault. It was her fault she died.*

When would she ever have another chance to ask her father the things she needed to know? She couldn't let him walk away, leaving this conversation unfinished. She couldn't let him leave without asking one thing. "Is that why you didn't want me anymore? Because you were mad at her?"

Kurt gazed into her face. "Rory Gorenzi, I *never* didn't want you."

"But you never came around to Gran's house. You wouldn't have anything to do with us."

"I didn't have the slightest idea what to do with a baby girl! But your grandmother did. And that was for the best."

"How can you possibly say that?" Rory exclaimed, forgetting where she was, forgetting the so far untouched glass of wine in her hands.

Kurt Gorenzi gave a crusty mountain-man smile. "Because, daughter, you've turned out so well." He met her eyes as he spoke, and she saw his sincerity.

Her heart sang. Her father moved away to speak to some newcomers, but she felt only joy. Her father was proud of her. He thought she'd turned out well. No, it hadn't been nice what he'd implied in regard to Seamus. But he cared, and he admired who she'd become. She couldn't remember ever feeling so happy. She couldn't wait for her grandmother to arrive at the open house so that she could discuss with Sondra some of the things her father had said—steering away, of course, from the subject of Rory's mother's and Sondra's daughter's infidelity.

Sondra *had* spoken of those things to her. But she didn't enjoy it. *He was a playboy, Rory,* she'd said of Kristen Gorenzi's lover. *A ski patrolman. He was all about skiing, and your mother, in that phase, was his counterpart. She wanted to be the best skier in Sultan.*

It sounded now, to Rory, a bit like Janine Jensen.

Abruptly, Rory remembered Lauren and her plan to find out about Silas. Lauren had disappeared, but Beau leaned against a doorjamb in the archway leading to the dining room. He looked dejected.

As Rory headed toward him, she couldn't help hearing again her father's heart-dampening words about Seamus. Somehow, they brought home to her just how much of her affection for Seamus's children was tied to their father's regard for her. Or that was how it seemed. Suddenly. Only because her father had said that Seamus wasn't and couldn't be serious about her. "Taken" with her, yes. Serious, no.

So what was she doing befriending these children? It wasn't part of her job, not twenty-four hours a day. Her job ended at approximately 5:00 p.m. every day.

But I like them.

And in a couple of months, they and their father would be gone from her life.

Her pleasure in her father's compliments now diminished by his uncomplimentary remarks, she approached Beau. "How's it going? You look bored out of your mind."

"I'm babysitting." He gestured toward the dining room floor, where Belle and Caleb were playing with giant Lego blocks the Realtor's crew had brought over.

"Are you getting paid?" Rory asked.

Beau shook his head. "They're my brother and sister. Anyhow, I get an allowance. We all do. It's for doing stuff like this."

Rory thought for a moment. "There are more games down in the basement. Have you ever played Nok-Hockey?"

Beau straightened up. "No. What is it?"

"Why don't you all come downstairs and we'll play."

SEAMUS GLANCED OUT an upstairs window. He admired the walnut sill and studied the streetlight below. Because it was on Sultan's most historic street the lamp was Victorian, as well. What would it be like to live in this town, perhaps in this showpiece of a home?

Rory had made clear that she wouldn't become romantically involved with a client of the Sultan Mountain School. That was a mature and reasonable stance, and Seamus applauded her for it. But what about when the course was over? He sensed she wouldn't discourage his attention then.

A figure paused under the lamplight. A young man in a stocking cap, the kind of loose clothing snowboarders wore, a warm jacket. As Seamus watched, another figure came to join him, and Seamus recognized his daughter Lauren.

Rory's warnings echoed in his head.

Yes, the boy was probably Silas. And yes, he should probably have asked Silas more questions, found out more.

The two weren't doing anything, just standing in the cold talking. After a brief time, the boy turned away and Lauren came back toward the house, though she looked back over her shoulder as she did so.

Maybe fourteen was too young to be dating.

Well, if so, it was a little late for him to do anything about it. Lauren had had her first "boyfriend" at the age of twelve. A boy in her class. Nothing about the situation, however silly it had seemed to Seamus, had worried him. But how old was Silas, really? Seamus had thought he was high school age. But not a senior. *I just didn't look at him that closely.*

He remembered why he hadn't. Because Lauren had been acting tough, acting the way she remembered Janine acting. *Any guy who tries taking advantage of me is going to wish he hadn't.*

Seamus had thought, *Yes, he will. Because of me.* Lauren had no self-defense training. She'd just been putting on the attitude, like a clone of her mother.

Seamus had been glad when Silas had arrived and he and Lauren left on foot to go have some dinner at the pizza place up the street.

I'm making a mess of things, he thought now. How could he lay down rules for Lauren's life if he was so afraid of another fight with her about Janine, so afraid of unleashing his own anger?

Yes, she was a good-enough student.

Yes, she was an athlete.

What was there to complain about in her behavior?

As long as Fiona's around, he thought.

But he had told Fiona he wanted to try getting on without her again—just for a time, just to see how it would go.

He rejoined the house tour. When it was over, he found Lauren talking to her friend, the barista. He joined them, and Lauren introduced him to Helena.

Helena was no high-school student. Seamus felt certain of that. College age, maybe, though she could be in her early to midtwenties. Helena looked at a mountaineering watch on her wrist and said, "See you, Lauren. At our place, if not before."

As she left, Seamus said, "Our place?"

"The coffeehouse," Lauren said. "She works there."

"That's its name?"

"Of course not."

"Her family owns it?"

The briefest hesitation. Yes, she was lying. About something. But she said, "No. Not that I know of."

"What do Silas's parents do in Sultan?"

"I haven't the slightest idea."

"You've met them?" Seamus asked.

"Actually, no."

"How old is Silas?"

Lauren looked at him squarely. "Why are you suddenly on this Twenty Questions About Silas kick?"

"I saw you talking to him out on the sidewalk. From an upstairs window."

"That wasn't even Silas. That was Jeremy."

"Who's Jeremy?"

"He works at the ski area. He's just a *friend*. I can have friends, can't I?"

Seamus felt outmaneuvered and wasn't sure why. He refused to be sidetracked. "How old, exactly, is Silas?"

"Exactly? Like, when's his birthday?"

"Years will do."

She shrugged. "He's, like, in high school."

Did the excessive use of *like* indicate lying? Seamus suspected so, in this case. "Like," he said, "what year in high school?"

"Um, probably about senior because he skipped a grade."

"He's out of school, isn't he?" Seamus said, deciding to sound, at this stage, as though it was no big deal.

She shrugged. "You know. Home school's kind of loose."

No, it's not, Seamus almost answered.

"He's here in Sultan with his family. Yes or no?"

She gave an exasperated sigh. "No, all right? He's got roommates. He's not, like, a criminal."

"If he wants to see you again," Seamus said, and now his daughter's face was red as she glanced around her to make sure they weren't being overheard, "he can come talk to me and explain why someone out of school is interested in dating a fourteen-year-old girl."

"Why wouldn't he be interested?"

Seamus didn't want to explain that most males in that general age group had more than kissing on the mind and going further with a fourteen-year-old was illegal. He wouldn't say this, because it wasn't okay with him for Lauren get that involved with any boy, and he didn't want to put the idea in her head. It just seemed *safer* not to explain.

And yet she'd asked.

I can't do this. I can't be both mother and father to this child.

"Let's talk about this at home," he suggested. Which at least bought him a little time. "Where are your brothers and sister?"

"I don't know." Shrug. "We're all just *friends*."

"You need friends your own age."

"You brought us here."

Seamus retreated into silence. He prowled the first floor without finding Beau, Caleb or Belle and finally decided they *might* be in the basement—which had not been on the house tour but which the Realtor had shown on request.

His children sat on the indoor-outdoor carpet in the basement, which was set up as a recreation room since Lola's departure. A three-by-five-foot board, small hockey sticks, wooden pucks. Belle was at one goal and Rory at the other, giving lots of encouragement.

"Nok-Hockey!" Seamus exclaimed. "I haven't seen this for years."

"It was my dad's, actually. A lot of his childhood toys ended up at my grandmother's house when I was a kid."

"He must have wanted you to have them."

She glanced up at him, and a range of emotions flickered in her eyes. A happiness at seeing him that seemed, just as quickly, to be extinguished, as if she'd just thought of something unpleasant or discouraging.

"Dad, play me!" Caleb said.

Seamus smiled and came to sit on the floor. "Well, first let me see what your sister can do."

As they played, he continued to observe Rory's changing mood. Pleasure at being with him was suddenly eclipsed by shadows he couldn't penetrate. As Seamus helped Belle, and Rory defended her goal with deliberate inattention, allowing the four-year-old to score, the boys chattered in the background, looking through the snake encyclopedia.

Beau said, "Now Seuss can come over, right? Because Lola's in Florida."

"Right," Rory agreed. "And it was never part of Lola's rules that she be allowed to wander all over the house. She had just escaped that time. Good job, Belle! You're winning."

"I'm glad she's gone," Beau said.

Me too, THOUGHT RORY.

The five of them lingered in the basement, Seamus playing a round first with Caleb and then with Beau. Finally, the kids trooped upstairs in search of gloves and mittens for the walk home, but their father lingered behind.

Rory couldn't forget any part of the conversation she'd had with *her* father. His reiteration of school policy. And his certainty that Seamus's designs on her were short-term.

"I just wanted to tell you," Seamus said, "that it seems you were right about Silas. Lauren has confessed that he's out of school."

"Out of high school?" Rory said, a little shocked in spite of herself. But things like that did happen—if parents let them.

"Yes. Lauren doesn't seem to fully grasp the picture. I'm not sure how to explain it to her."

You're not going to push this conversation off on me, Rory thought indignantly. But the feeling was laced with hurt connected to her father's assessment of Seamus's intentions. If Seamus just wanted to, well, *use* her as a girlfriend and a buffer between himself and his children... No. Just no.

She said, "I'm sure the right words will come to you."

Then she turned and climbed the stairs.

CHAPTER EIGHT

IN THE MIDDLE of March came the first of the Sultan Mountain School tests for Seamus and his family, so that all of them could earn certificates saying they'd completed their course work. Rory would have liked to make the one-day expedition of skiing and orienteering a family activity, but it wasn't possible. Seamus, as an adult, would need to be challenged more than his family.

As luck would have it, Rory was assigned as his companion for the day's skiing, which would take them up onto Cone Mountain and through the ghost town of Gypsum over a twelve-mile course, provided they didn't get lost.

The morning of the nineteenth, Rory and Seamus set out in her car for Jackson Gulch. From there they would ascend Cone Mountain with climbing skins on, then ski over to

Gypsum and in a loop over a mountain pass and back down to the vehicle. Rory hoped.

As she drove, she mentally double-checked everything she'd brought. She always kept a list in her pack so that she'd forget nothing when she set out on a ski trip, but it didn't stop her from trying to imagine possible emergencies of every sort and then thinking of all the things that would be needed to return them home safely.

When they reached their parking space near the foot of Jackson Gulch and began unloading the car, preparing to don skis and packs, Rory said, "This isn't a *test,* per se. It's just a requirement for getting your certificate."

"I understand."

It wasn't the day Rory would have chosen for the expedition. Snow was already falling, two feet expected with the storm. But it was Sultan Mountain School policy to pick a date and make do with the weather. She watched as Seamus briefly consulted the topography, then showed her the route he'd planned the night before. "This is how we'll go if avalanche conditions allow," he told her.

"Fine."

She let him lead off, but he seemed reluctant to plunge ahead, so for a while they skied side-by-side. Then they took turns breaking trail.

Breaking trail on skis going uphill was exhausting work, but Rory knew that they must keep moving to achieve their goal in daylight. Though it was only beginning to lighten as they skied away from her car, they had a long way to go. Also, she had one of her unsettled feelings about this trip; an unspoken fear that they might run into trouble before its end.

They skied for two hours and made good time. When they paused at their first landmark—a ski hut owned by the Sultan Mountain School—and stopped inside for a quick bite to eat, Seamus finally said, "Rory, how would you feel about seeing me once the course is over?"

Seeing me. Yes, somehow it did sound temporary. But they'd never dated. Dating meant trying things out, seeing how people got along. Dating didn't mean that Seamus Lee wanted a casual fling with her. It didn't mean he wanted even that much. A date was a date.

"I'd go out with you," she said, "but let's

not talk about it until the course is over, all right? Let's conclude *this* relationship first." She changed the subject, her father's warnings about Seamus's intentions still ringing in her ears. "At least we'll have some nice powder for all the downhill."

They put their packs and skis back on, and Seamus checked their bearings again before they set out, still heading uphill. "This is a great adventure," Seamus exclaimed. "I bet it clears up later, too. Beacon on?" he asked her.

Rory checked, though she'd never turned it off. "Yes."

The day did clear, slowly, and before they started their descent down the other side of Cone Mountain, Seamus dug an avalanche pit and evaluated the findings. He made a grim face as both he and Rory watched a slab separate in the layers he'd dug. "Well," he said, "we could go back the way we came. Or we could go on. On either side, the conditions won't be good, but we can avoid more paths if we go back the way we came."

Rory said nothing, waiting for him to make the call and hoping she wouldn't have to overrule it.

"Better safe than sorry," he said. "Back to the car. We'll have to do this another day."

But as far as Rory was concerned, Seamus had just earned his certificate.

She smiled. "Let's go."

"After you."

She went ahead of him, gliding down the slope they'd climbed, following the fall line, gracefully carving her first telemark turn and coming out of it even as she heard the whisper.

It was sometimes possible to ski out of an avalanche by pressing the heels down. She knew this anecdotally and now she attempted it as she headed for the side, away from the path of the slide. It caught her, and she could not keep her heels down, so she swam, focusing on everything she knew. Swim for the top, swim for the top, make a path around your face, swim for the top. And before the snow stopped, in those last moments, she must make a strong thrust and kick hard. Through white, not water. She wasn't sure what was happening, except that she and Seamus were far enough from help that she was in trouble.

HE WATCHED HER and kept his eyes fixed on the last place he'd seen her even as the snow settled, which seemed to take forever. He skied down along beside the chute thinking, No, no, no. He stopped further up slope than he'd last seen her and set his beacon to Receive.

He found her signal much sooner and more easily than he'd anticipated and made his way slowly and carefully toward it, across the avalanche path.

He saw a glove. Moving.

"Yes, Rory!" he called. She had kept a hand above the surface. He reached her, got out of his skis, and began shoveling with his small avalanche shovel. He carefully followed her arm, then saw the bright yellow of her helmet and cleared the snow from her face. She spit out snow, saying, "I'm pretty sure I broke my other wrist—I felt the crack. I think I heard it, but I couldn't have."

The injured arm was her left, and he was thankful for that small favor as he continued digging her out.

She helped as much as she was able, saying, "I'm fine, I'm alive. This is good. Thank you, Seamus. Thank you, Seamus," as if by continuing to talk she would minimize her own peril. Then, a groan, as they discovered that she'd lost a ski.

"It's worth a little time digging for it right where we are," Rory said, "but we're probably out of luck." *She* was out of luck and out a pair of Sultan custom telemark skis, which started at seven hundred dollars. Also, it was going to be a long trek back, even as far as the hut, on the one small pair of snowshoes they had between them. But at least they had those.

Seamus set to work with his shovel, and Rory poked around with hers, using only her right arm.

But half an hour later, she still had just one ski and no poles. "I can snowshoe," she said. In telemark boots, which would be a unique form of torture. "You ski, and I'll go as fast as I can, but don't go out of sight of me."

"Why don't you ski and I'll snowshoe?"

"No. I'm lighter—the shoes will work better for me."

Seamus helped her strap the lone ski, which she said they should take with them— they weren't home yet, and it might prove useful—to her pack.

As she trudged back down toward the hut, following Seamus, who skied for a hundred yards, then waited at a tree, she regretted not having dug a snow pit earlier to check the avalanche conditions. She wouldn't have suggested it overtly, not at first. She would have just done something to make Seamus think of the idea for himself. But neither of them had thought of it.

At least it was spring, rather than early winter or fall before the winter solstice. As it was, she decided optimistically, unwilling to acknowledge the blisters she was definitely going to have from wearing boots not made for snowshoeing, they might make it to the car by dark.

But they were behind the mountain, and it quickly grew cold in the shade. Rory made herself keep walking, pretending the heat from her blisters was spreading through her limbs. Pretending the cold felt good on her injured forearm. The arm didn't hurt, except at the wrist; she couldn't turn it.

Repeatedly, Seamus asked how she was, until she snapped, "Why don't you ask that just once every half hour?"

It was late afternoon. They had not yet

reached the hut, but at least they could see their old tracks. Rory worried they'd gone past it, but Seamus pointed out a ponderosa pine he'd noticed on the way up and said that the tree was above the hut.

I do not want to spend the night in that hut.

It wasn't exactly a cozy retreat. There was no firewood or coal for the stove, no food. It was shelter and not much more, and Rory knew the insulation was practically nonexistent. Not to mention that it was tucked beneath the trees and received little natural heat from the sun.

But she'd had the miles trudging down, sinking a foot with every step, to remember that there was no moon. They couldn't walk without moonlight, and she wouldn't send him on without her for many reasons. No, she and Seamus Lee were doomed to spend the night in that hut, while his children worried about him, and she would have the chance to analyze everything about herself that defined her as a complete screwup. To be caught in an avalanche!

When they finally reached the hut, it was almost dark, and Seamus was as cold as she was.

"So," he said, "I think we have a cold night ahead."

"Yes. But I have a stove so we can melt water and make hot drinks. And I have a sleeping bag."

"I don't," he said. "I didn't think…"

"I know. It wasn't on your list. You have an emergency blanket, right, and so do I. We'll share and make do." It was just survival, not romantic, not any of the things outlawed by the policies of the Sultan Mountain School. She carried her compressed lightweight sleeping bag routinely on day-long excursions, because she'd never been able to get past the image of staying out all night, perhaps, with only an emergency blanket. Seamus, she realized now, should really have been carrying a sleeping bag, too, but the school didn't suggest it for such a short trip.

Well, now they would make do, as she'd said. "What about your kids?"

He was frowning. "I've been thinking of that ever since I realized how late it is. I think Lauren will check with SMS. She'll go to the school and tell them we haven't returned."

"Well, *I'm* supposed to check in there, too,"

Rory said. "They'll realize we're missing. I just hope someone thinks of the kids."

"They will."

She would gratefully have climbed into her sleeping bag and remained there alone, cinching the hood around her head. Instead, she and Seamus rummaged in the cupboards and did find the hut's supply of emergency blankets, which would certainly make the night a little more comfortable. Needless to say, the other thing that would help was body heat. Snuggling up together.

They peeled out of their outer clothes, and hung them up to dry on the ends of the bunk beds.

"Lower bunk?" Seamus said.

"Thank you. Then, maybe I can manage not to break anything else."

She'd no doubt she'd need his help getting back into her ski pants and jacket the next morning. Now she felt dirty in her wool-and-silk long underwear. Her wrist and forearm had swelled noticeably.

"Should we make a splint?" Seamus asked.

"I have an Ace bandage in my first-aid kit," she said. "That would probably help."

In the light of his headlamp, he dug in her

pack until he found her first-aid kit. He had brought a stove, too. And they would certainly have enough fuel to keep them supplied with water and hot drinks through the night.

There were awkward moments as Seamus, also in long johns, climbed onto the hard mattress of the lower bunk with her. Rory attempted to cover him with part of the sleeping bag. "We'll wrap all the blankets around us tonight," she said.

"My dream come true."

"Not mine," she muttered. "Don't take it personally. Just… Getting hit by a slide is not my idea of a great adventure."

But she had to admit that being this close to Seamus… His firm thigh brushed her leg and, even though they were both clothed, blood rushed through her, hot and tingling.

She noted the cragginess of his face as he found the bandage, unrolled it, gently pulled up the sleeve of her long undershirt and began to wrap her forearm, wrist and hand. Without looking at her, he said, "You're so different from Janine."

"How so?" She let him take her arm, watched his strong long fingers with the bandage. Thought about how close they were to each other.

Seamus carefully turned her arm, saying, "Tell me if it hurts."

"That does. I don't want to turn my wrist that way."

"Okay. I can do it in this direction." He began wrapping the injury with a skill that suggested he'd done similar things before.

Carryover from the first-aid course he'd taken with the school? Rory wondered.

"Janine was caught in an avalanche once. I wasn't with her. She actually broke her femur. But she was proud of the incident. As far as she was concerned, it was a war story to be told and retold."

"Only where I'm unknown," Rory said. "I find it humiliating."

"I'm glad you kept that hand up."

"I was trying to do everything I could to get to the surface. I thought I could ski out of it, but no way." He had started to talk about his wife, Rory reminded herself. And she wanted to know about Janine Jensen. "When was Janine's avalanche experience?" she asked.

"Five or six years before she died. I think

Lauren was in kindergarten." His expression was both grim and sad.

Rory watched his profile, waiting for him to say more. There was nothing she could think to say to encourage him. Not *Boy, it really sounds as though you didn't like your wife very much.* Or, *I bet she wasn't easy to live with.*

"Have I told you," she asked at last, "that Samantha worked for her?"

"Samantha herself reminded me of the connection. I don't know if I was ever introduced to her back then, but I definitely remembered her face." He shook his head. "The women at the resource center thought Janine should have been canonized."

Rory lifted her eyebrows.

"I mean, they didn't think she was saintly in all her relationships, just that what she did for the resource center was saintly."

"And were you the bad guy?" Rory asked.

He considered, then shook his head. "Probably to Janine sometimes. But no one would ever have suspected me of hurting her. I think they knew she'd never put up with that."

"Or that you're the kind of person who wouldn't behave that way."

He gave a rueful smile. "You know the worst part?"

She shook her head.

"That there were times—it wasn't as straightforward as me wishing she was dead. But sometimes, just for a minute or two, I wished she would cease to be a problem to me. That she'd fall in love with someone else and a divorce would be *her* idea."

"Did you ever talk about divorce?"

He shook his head. "No. Well, maybe obliquely. About the gun, for instance. She'd say things like, *You're not telling me what to do. That won't fly.*"

"And you? What did you say?"

"That I didn't want my children living in the same house with a gun." He finished wrapping Rory's arm, fastened it with clips and lifted it gently to his lips. Then glanced at her impishly. "Just part of the medical treatment. Belle says wounds don't heal if they aren't kissed."

"Then how did she get over her scrapes before she came to Sultan?" Rory realized too late that this was one of her instances of speaking without thinking. And there was no taking it back, making it better.

"Fiona," Seamus said, not looking pleased with himself. He moved away. "Let's see if I can get my stove going, and we can have something hot to drink." He reached for his ski pants and dragged them on over his long underwear, since they'd dried out.

She tried to think of something besides how much she liked being close to him, but could only reflect on the fact that she'd practically come out and said that when he came to Sultan he'd been a virtual stranger to his own children. *Think first, Rory.*

"When you go back to Telluride," she asked, "will Fiona still work for you?"

"I'm not sure we're going back to Telluride. Not to stay."

She heard the hiss of gas and saw the ring of flame appear. He stepped outside the hut and then came back in, his camping pot filled with snow.

She considered everything her father had said the night of the open house. Her father believed that if she became involved with Seamus and the relationship failed, Seamus would desert Sultan. Otherwise—if she left him alone, in other words—he might become a permanent resident.

And here I am alone with him at night in this ski hut. If I make a wrong move, Seamus will take his money and his children and go back to Telluride.

Her father would be disappointed in her.

Not to mention the fact that Seamus was a client.

But what happened in this hut on this night would be no one's business but theirs.

Rory tried to feel comfortable with the conclusion. But in the back of her mind there was a set of scales. On one side was what she felt for Seamus and the possibility that he liked her, too—and that his feelings for her *weren't* temporary. On the other side was her father and her desire to please him by making a success of her job at the Sultan Mountain School—and by behaving in such a way that Seamus and his family would settle permanently in Sultan. As if she alone could dictate that outcome.

As if a bad experience with her would be sufficient to negate that outcome.

As if, by *not* becoming involved with Seamus, she could ensure that he *would* move to Sultan.

Was it possible that her father simply

wanted to protect her? Maybe he saw Seamus as the kind of man who could never settle down.

But no, that wasn't it.

Seamus had been married to an attorney.

She, Rory, had completed one year of college, and had no great desire to return to school. Her lack of a college education had never before made her feel inferior, but now it did.

Seamus made hot cocoa, and Rory drank hers quickly, grateful for the calories and the warmth. She tucked her water bottle inside the sleeping bag with her to keep it from freezing. Seamus stepped outside briefly, then came back in and said, "I may as well join you, so we can both keep warm. Is this all right, Rory?"

"It's necessary, is what it is," she said, evading the question. Trying not to think about just how much she wanted him beside her.

As he slipped into the nest they'd made, tucking the blankets around them both, he said, "I just know that you've sent one message about..." He let the sentence hang unfinished.

Her father's warning lurked, like a visitor outstaying his welcome. She tried to push it away.

Seamus lay on his side facing her, barely visible in the starlight that filtered through the dirty windows. "I'm surprised you don't have a boyfriend. You must have men pursuing you."

"Oh. Sometimes new people. We all sort of already know each other in Sultan. And romance hasn't been a priority for me." *Until now.*

"Why is that?"

"Well, I've had friends who really want to be part of a couple—you know, with anybody. But I tend to wait until someone really catches my attention."

"How does a man do that?"

She didn't know how to answer him. Working at the Sultan Mountain School was not just a way for her to make money. It was a way to win her father's approval. And she felt she was doing that.

Yes, Seamus had her attention. But she wasn't sure she could afford it. Should she be candid with him and tell him what her father had said? "My father has discouraged me from becoming involved with you."

Seamus caught his breath. Then he raised his head, propping himself up with his forearm. "Did he." It wasn't a question.

"He feels I'm not right for you. He pointed out—with reason, I think—that you're worldly and well-educated and I'm basically a high-school graduate who has spent her life in Sultan, Colorado." Why not tell him everything? "He believes that any interest you feel in me will be passing."

He said nothing.

"It doesn't mean he doesn't like you or value you," she said quickly. Oh, boy, what if she'd messed everything up? *By talking too much, Rory!* What if she'd colored Seamus's whole experience at the Sultan Mountain School with this burst of frankness? "He just doesn't want me to get in over my head, or abilities, or experience or any of that. It really wasn't anything negative about you."

They were using her down jacket as a pillow. She changed position, fluffing the jacket and grabbing her ski pants to add to the pillow.

Seamus inhaled the scent of her on her jacket and in her hair. He'd never met a woman so alluring. But clearly, Kurt Gorenzi doubted his intentions. And why wouldn't he? Seamus had lost a wife to a violent death. That was enough to make any father skittish. And Kurt seemed to sense something of Seamus's ambivalent feelings about his role as a parent to his four children.

Yes, Kurt had been right to warn his daughter. He'd been caring and protective. Seamus hoped that Rory appreciated that fact.

His hand strayed to her hair, in its messy braid. He felt the ridges of curls, then slid his hand to the curve of her cheek.

Her head fell back against the jacket and her chin lifted toward him.

His mouth felt for hers and touched it. She returned his kiss, gently, somehow purely.

The kiss deepened, and he felt feverishly warm, so that the frigid air in the hut was welcome.

He said, "Are you going to heed your father's warning?"

Slowly, her head moved. Minutely. First to

one side, then the other. A single-word answer: *No.*

The words came from him in a rush. "When I see you with my children, it's perfect. I want you there. Nobody's ever been so right."

She said, "I love them. I love them all, but please don't mistake wanting a mother for your children for wanting a partner for yourself. It's not the same. You have Fiona. And there are *many* people who are good with kids and who can be paid to be good with kids. You don't need to marry someone for that."

"Rory, I *need* a partner. I believe you can be that person. I believe we can…" He heard himself; knew he was jumping forward. He'd barely kissed this woman. And yet he knew that she was the woman he wanted. Everything she represented *fit.*

"Slow down," she said. "This is crazy." And she felt herself going crazy, too; crazy for a man who *was* a man, not a boy who spent his life backcountry skiing, someone who lived only to play, as her previous boyfriends had done. She'd hated that characteristic, hated seeing adult males behave as though there was nothing more important than the next run. Seamus was different.

But caution wrapped itself around her. Caution penetrated the overwhelming desire to kiss him again. Caution said that if she acted on the desire she might *feel* too much. That it might be too late, then.

Seamus held himself back from her. "We're not going to get any sleep," he said.

"Why don't you take the emergency blankets and go up on the top bunk?"

"Okay." He sat up, beginning to gather the blankets.

Immediately, she regretted the decision. But she didn't really *know* him. And yet she did. The things she didn't know were things she couldn't ask. It would be insensitive and wrong to ask.

She said, "I'm sorry. I'm apologizing in advance. Samantha said you were the one who found Janine."

"Yes. She'd been hit in the throat." His voice had turned cold. "Her eyes were open. Is that what you wanted to know?"

"I want to know *you* and somehow I don't feel as if I can, when there's so much I *don't* know."

"It was three-thirty in the afternoon. The kids were going to be home in minutes. That was all I could think about, and she was in the mudroom, where the washer and dryer are. I grabbed towels and threw them over her, so that her body was covered, and then I went and stood in the door of the mudroom so no one could go in and I called 911 on my cell phone."

"Were the police upset that you touched things?"

"They understood why I'd done it."

"What happened when the kids came home? Did they show up before the police?"

"They did. It had been snowing. I told Lauren and Beau that they had to shovel the front walk. They knew something was wrong. They wanted to go past me, but I yelled at them to get shoveling."

"Where were Caleb and Belle?"

"With Fiona, in town. Beau and Lauren wanted a snack, which was reasonable, and so I was shouting at them when the police came. Then I told them their mother was dead."

Rory's hand tightened on his wrist. She

knew, he realized, that this had been the worst part. Then, telling Caleb.

"Lauren screamed. Beau ran around to the far side of the house. Lauren wanted to see her, but I wouldn't let her. One of the cops helped me with her."

"Oh, no."

"Yes."

"And they never saw her?" Rory asked.

"Not until later. After they'd…worked on her. At the funeral home."

Rory had felt she did not know him. But now she realized she *had* known him. Everything he'd done was what she'd have expected of him.

"There were scenes," he said. "In the next few days. The kids were a mess. Lauren and Beau, especially. I was so lucky to have Fiona. I don't know what she said to them. I know she helped them write down their feelings in poems. And she read to them. She used to take them outside a lot, to walk and talk. She'd talk about everything being connected through the earth. About how ancient the mountains were. It helped. They seemed to accept that their mother had become a lasting part of the earth. I don't understand how she did it. Maybe I've deluded myself, thinking that she was successful in helping them through their grieving."

"Who helped you?"

He exhaled slowly, looking straight ahead. "I didn't grieve for Janine. I grieved for my children because their mother had died and I knew they could hardly bear it. I hated Janine for being so stupid." Rory's hand had found his, and now he said, "Funny. Talking about it now, I feel less angry at her. It was a disaster, and I know I should let go of her part in it."

"I'm not sure 'should' is a practical word in this situation."

Seamus lightly touched her injured left arm. "How's this?"

"Not bad, unless I move around. I can tell it's swelling. Seamus, thank you for talking about all this to me. I needed to know about you. The history."

"That makes sense. I'd like to know more of yours, too."

She laughed ruefully. "To be perfectly honest, my recent history has had to do with employment—getting fired from jobs. It's not all that interesting."

"Fired?"

"Yes."

"What was it like growing up with your grandmother?"

Rory considered. "It was different. It was always a little sad—I thought my father didn't want me."

Did she imagine it or did he flinch?

Rory rushed on. "But my grandmother was good. She would talk with me about anything. The only thing she didn't like to discuss was the fact that my mother had cheated on my dad. Also, she seemed to think the man involved was not worth it in any way. She said my mom had trouble getting anyone to reach her soul—because she was so into plants, into science. My dad said something like that, too. He implied that he couldn't keep up with her intellectually, or in terms of life experience. But my mom's always going to be a mystery to me."

She changed the subject. "Seamus, this might be something you can't do or don't want to do. But…" She hunted for an analogy. "I love Desert, but you've probably guessed that she wasn't always the easiest person to live with or be friends with."

"I've guessed that," he agreed.

"It always helps me if I think of the things I really love about her, the times when she's been at her best as a human being. For example, sometimes she's so *caring*. I mean, there were occasions when I felt just rotten and she knew exactly how to say the right thing."

He listened quietly.

"I hope this isn't stupid to suggest, but maybe you could do that with Janine. And then you'd have something positive to tell the kids about her. I know you want them to love her memory. Otherwise, you wouldn't worry about losing your temper around them."

"You're wise beyond your years, Rory Gorenzi." He stroked her hair.

She said, "You can stay here."

CHAPTER NINE

"RORY! SEAMUS!"

A sweeping light flashed outside and a deep voice penetrated the darkness.

Rory awoke, immediately felt her throbbing arm, remembered where she was, knew Seamus was beside her and identified his scent, his closeness.

Seamus quickly rose from the lower bunk and grabbed his ski pants to pull on over his long johns.

Although they'd done nothing more than kiss, cuddle and sleep, Rory grabbed the emergency blankets from the lower bunk and dragged them onto the top bunk. She didn't want her dad speculating.

Watching her, Seamus bit back a smile. He opened the cabin door. "We're here."

Two figures skied closer in the dark. Kurt Gorenzi and an SMS instructor, Carrie Wayne. "*He* was going to come up here alone looking for you," Carrie said, as they released their skis. She was forty-five or so and had lived in Sultan only a year. Rory liked her and envied the way in which she always seemed to be organized and ready for anything.

"What happened?" Kurt asked, never looking at Seamus, only at his daughter.

Seamus lit his headlamp and set it on the top bunk to provide light.

"A slide. I got buried. Seamus dug me out. I think I broke my wrist."

While Seamus asked where his children were and Carrie explained that one of the instructors was staying at the house with them, Kurt went into mountain-man first-aid mode, concentrating entirely on Rory's injury. He removed the bandaging and produced a splint from his pack, while Carrie set to work melting snow.

"You didn't have to come," Rory said.

Her father made no reply.

She winced, not at the pain in her wrist but at the blisters she'd gotten from snowshoeing in her telemark boots.

Carrie said, "Oh, right, like he's not going to go looking for his own daughter."

I never didn't want you, Kurt had said.

"Tell me about this slide," he requested now.

And Rory realized that he expected an avalanche report. He wanted her to describe the type of avalanche and the elevation of the start zone, estimated width and running length, aspect of the path, size of the avalanche relative to its path, triggering mechanism, weather conditions and so on. She said, "Slab."

Seamus interrupted, "She was in it. She didn't see it." And he described when and how it happened and what he'd seen from the top. "It was about fifty feet across. She skied for the side and then swam to the top. Or I imagine that's what you did, Rory." He described digging her out, searching for her skis and poles and the long trek back to the hut.

Rory gratefully took the cup of instant chai that Carrie handed her.

Kurt said, "Well, we have a toboggan outside, and we're prepared to take you out of here."

At night? Rory thought. "What time is it?"

Carrie consulted her watch. "Three-fifteen."

"I'd prefer to make it down on my own

power," Rory said. *I just wish I had a different pair of boots...or some skis.*

"It's steep. I don't think you should do it with a broken wrist. If you were a client, I wouldn't allow it." Her father sounded both matter-of-fact and angry.

"I'm sorry," Rory said. "It was my fault. I should have suggested digging a pit before we got up that far."

"Conditions might have changed before you reached the top." Her father shrugged. "It sounds as though Seamus did well."

"Phenomenally," Rory said. He had saved her life.

"Well, I think *I'll* head back down," her father said. "You do as you want. We'll see you by...say, noon?"

Rory hesitated, then nodded.

"Why did it take you so long to get down to this hut?" Kurt asked.

"Well, I'm snowshoeing in my tele boots," Rory explained.

Kurt considered this. "I'll leave you my skis and poles and snowshoe down."

"Do you have decent boots?" Rory asked. Then she saw that he was wearing his reliable old leather telemark boots, not high-tech plastic ones like hers.

"Yes," he answered emphatically.

HE AND CARRIE STAYED for another twenty minutes, then left.

Rory watched them go and said, "This is bad."

"What?" Seamus asked.

"That I had to be rescued. I hate that—I really hate it. And I got injured. It's bad."

Seamus's thoughts were elsewhere. What did Kurt think of Seamus and his daughter spending the night here together? Well, he'd accepted it, just as he'd accepted Rory's decision to remain in the hut rather than leave by toboggan.

He said, "You know something?"

"What?"

"Janine would have taken that toboggan ride."

Rory barely heard him.

THEY REACHED HER CAR at ten the next morning, and Seamus drove them back to Sultan while Rory checked her cell phone messages. There was one from Desert, saying that things were still going well in Florida, that she was actually enjoying her father's company but wanted to complain to someone about the environment of her parents' home. Then, a message from Rory's father.

"Rory, you've got an appointment at the clinic as soon as you return. Dr. Hennessey will be waiting for you. He thinks he can take care of your wrist here in Sultan."

The Sultan clinic was spartan, the doctor a semiretired general practitioner who'd moved to Sultan from Aspen. Rory realized her father must have contacted him earlier that morning.

When Seamus dropped her at the clinic, she found her grandmother waiting. Sondra Nichols was turned out in high fashion, as usual, in black wool pants, high-heeled boots and white fur. As Rory walked through the door, she said, "There you are. I *hope* this teaches you that backcountry skiing is *dangerous*."

Rory kissed her and then greeted Dr. Hennessey, who examined and X-rayed her wrist and found the crack at the distal end of her ulna. Seamus had gone on with her car to the Empire Street house to see how his children were. Rory's mind was on them, too. She was enormously glad that after finding Seamus and Rory, her father had been able to return to Sultan and reassure the kids.

As the doctor fit a splint to her wrist, Samantha burst through the door. "I cannot *believe* you," she exclaimed. "An *avalanche?* I'm kind of jealous, in a way. That you survived an avalanche."

"It was hideous," Rory said. Skiing down from the hut, she'd remembered the sensation of being buried, of knowing that her life was in the hands of her companion. Before Seamus had reached her, she'd tried to dig herself out, but she'd had only one arm to use, and it had been wedged above her.

Her grandmother left to collect her mail at the post office, but Samantha remained with Rory, and then the two friends walked home together, Rory in three pairs of socks, having left the torturing tele boots in her car. Right now, she preferred socks as footwear, even in the cold.

Samantha said, "Is something going on between you and Seamus?"

"Yes, and I don't know if my father figured that out last night. He warned me against getting involved." She told Samantha the things her father had said and acknowledged the dilemma of Seamus being a client.

"Well, guess what."

Rory looked at her. "What?"

"Our house is already under contract."

"To who?"

"One of the Telluride investors your father brought to the open house. I don't think he plans to live in it, and he doesn't want renters. I think he wants to turn it into a saloon, with rooms upstairs."

Rory groaned.

"We have thirty days," Samantha said. "Until closing. We can stay at the hot springs after that."

"The hot springs is just a temporary solution. We need to look for another house to rent." And the rent, Rory knew, would be substantially more than she'd paid all the years she'd lived in the house that Desert owned.

"Your dad said to come by the school 'at your leisure.'"

Rory's vague uneasiness intensified. Her broken wrist would restrict her usefulness to the Sultan Mountain School. Plus, now she was involved with a client. She felt almost as if she'd become part of Seamus during the night they'd spent together kissing, talking and feeling.

So, must she walk away from her job? The Lees would soon be finished with their time at the Sultan Mountain School. Just a few more weeks.

How did I let something like this happen?

Well, they'd just have to be discreet and a bit reserved for the next few weeks.

"Worried about your dad?" Samantha seemed to read her mind.

"Funny. You've called him that twice. Other people call him that and I never think of him that way. He's my father, but Dad sounds as if he's actually part of my life."

Samantha nodded sympathetically.

Rory said, "He did come out last night, though. But that's who he is. He would have done it for any of the instructors, for any of the clients—for anyone."

Samantha glanced at her. They had almost reached the house when Rory spotted Beau walking toward her with Seuss. "Rory!" he shouted.

The story Seamus had told her the night

before of Janine's death came to the front of her mind. "I'm glad to see you," she exclaimed. "But I have to get inside before the cold gets through these socks."

He followed the women up the path to the massive pink Victorian and came inside. The puppy began sniffing the floor, the furniture, skidding on the wood and wagging his tail.

Rory said, "I'm so sorry that happened, Beau. All of you must have been terrified when your dad didn't get back."

Beau shrugged. "I didn't think anything bad had happened. I mean, nothing that bad's going to happen to us *again*."

Rory hoped that was true. In any case, she wasn't going to discourage his optimistic attitude.

"I thought he might have gotten you lost or something, but I knew you'd figure it out."

His blind faith in her abilities both humbled and alarmed her. "It's a dangerous world out there, Beau."

"I want to hear about the avalanche."

They sat in the kitchen drinking milk and eating some cookies left over from a party at the hot springs. Rory told Samantha and Beau about the avalanche. "I was lucky," she concluded. "Very lucky. We should have been more careful. That's how accidents happen." She realized, as she spoke it, that the word *accident* might make Beau think of his mother's death. That hadn't been her intention.

He said, "Yeah," and then said nothing more.

HER FATHER STOOD UP from his desk when she entered his office.

She grabbed one of the old wooden chairs with a leather seat and back, and sat down.

Kurt walked behind her, closed the door and returned to his desk.

Rory tensed.

"So," he said, "in light of your injury, I'm going to put you on some clerical work. We've got paperwork to file, other tasks, some letters to write. Think you can do that? I realize you have only your dominant hand to work with."

Rory said, "Thank you. I'm *sorry,*" she repeated. "I'm sorry I let this happen."

He cracked a smile and shook his head. "When you're in the backcountry, accidents can happen. Fortunately, this one had a happy ending."

Rory hesitated. "So...someone else will finish up as the Lee family's program coordinator and head instructor?"

"In consultation with you. But it's not realistic for you to take the kids on their field exams. They've done the course work. I'd say your job is pretty well done. You did it well. Let's move you into some other functions here at the school, so that you can get a better idea of the whole picture."

Rory could hardly believe her ears. It sounded almost as if he was grooming her for a position of greater responsibility. If he wanted her to "get a better idea of the whole picture." "Thank you," she said. "Thank you."

"I'm going to set you up in Carrie's office, and she's going to show you some of the things she's been responsible for." He rose from his chair again. "I want to give you another day to rest from your accident. Tomorrow, 8:00 a.m.?"

"Yes," Rory said.

BELLE GAZED DISTRUSTFULLY at Jay Norris, the instructor who'd looked after them the night before and who would now be taking each of them into the field. Watching his daughter, Seamus reminded himself that Belle would be demonstrating her skiing technique along with the other children from her ski class. Rory had been by to formally hand the reins to Jay and to discuss the change with the whole family. Then, she'd left, to give Jay a chance to organize their activities.

He was a decent young man, and Seamus picked up the fact that he'd briefly been Desert's boyfriend.

Belle said, "I want Rory to test me."

Jay crouched beside her. "I know. But Rory got hurt in the avalanche, so she has to take a break from being out in the field. I'm sorry, Belle. You've got to put up with me."

She turned to Seamus and wrapped her arms around his legs.

Lauren, lying on the couch, abruptly sat up. "Well, I'm free for right now. Correct, Jay?"

"You are. This afternoon at about two, I want you to fill out an evaluation of the school, but your field exam isn't until tomorrow."

Lauren picked up her pale blue ski jacket and pulled it on.

"Where are you off to?" Seamus asked. Ever since the open house, he'd tried to keep closer tabs on Lauren and what she was doing. But they always seemed to walk a fine line. He did not want to restrict her too much and risk another argument about her mother. Yet he knew she was spending time with people he believed were too old for her. He resisted saying, *No, you can't go.*

"The coffeehouse," she said.

He checked his coat pockets and found a ten-dollar bill. "Bring me back a cappuccino?" he asked. "And yours is on me."

She made a face. "I want to hang out there."

"So, bring my coffee back first." That would take up some time, Seamus reasoned. Time she might otherwise use less wisely.

Lauren sighed dramatically. "All right."

Jay glanced at her as she went out the door, his expression thoughtful.

Seamus said, "Yes?" with the sense that he was about to learn more about how his oldest daughter spent her free time.

Jay glanced at Belle, the only other person in the room, and then stood up. Seamus could well imagine that even if the other man knew something, he would be reluctant to speak—

most of all, to Seamus. Seamus tried to think of some way to make it possible for Jay to reveal what, if anything, he knew about Lauren's hours away from the rest of her family.

Jay said, "How old is she?"

"Fourteen, going on twenty-five," Seamus said.

Jay nodded thoughtfully. He didn't answer.

"Why?" Seamus asked.

"Some kids I know—from the ski area—are under the impression she's sixteen."

Seamus's eyes widened. So he'd never needed to explain to Lauren why she shouldn't be interesting to a twenty-year-old male. Lauren, perhaps, already knew. And she'd told the male—or males—that she was already sixteen. The age of legal consent.

"Thank you," Seamus said. "Can I count on you to circulate the real facts?"

The young man grinned. "Definitely."

RORY SELDOM WENT out for coffee. When she drank coffee, it was black coffee brewed at home. But her more than satisfactory meeting with her father called for a celebration, so she walked to Sultan's one real coffeehouse, Grounds for Action, to order a two-shot caffe latte.

When she walked inside, the first person she saw was Lauren, sitting near the wood-stove with two backcountry skiers and another girl. Rory knew none of them, but she could tell at a glance that they were all several years older than Lauren.

This is not my responsibility.

Yet Lauren was Seamus's daughter. And Rory cared about Lauren in her own right. "What are you doing? Are you off work today, then?" Lauren asked, when Rory walked up to her.

Rory nodded. "I'm getting a latte."

"Will you take my dad's to him? I ordered him one and they're making it."

"Actually, I can't," Rory improvised. It would be unwise for her to return to Seamus's house right now. Jay was the Lees' program coordinator and he needed to be supported as such.

But the door swung open behind her, and in came Seamus, with Belle. Rory knew that Caleb and Beau must be skiing, demonstrating technique as part of their fieldwork.

"I thought I'd come after that cup of coffee myself."

"She's making it," Lauren told him. She remained near Rory and Seamus, and Rory suspected this was so that she wouldn't have to introduce the people with whom she'd been sitting.

Seamus swept the coffeehouse as if looking for someone. "I don't see your friend, the barista."

"It's her day off," Lauren said.

Seamus seemed alert to everyone present in the long, narrow shop. He'd spotted the group near the woodstove, noticed them glancing at Lauren and had undoubtedly picked up that they were her friends.

"So," Seamus said, "I hear that you're sixteen."

Color flooded Lauren's face and Rory moved away, doing her best to pretend she hadn't heard this. She crouched to speak with Belle.

Belle said, "I want hot chocolate. Dad said."

Dad. Good job, Seamus. He was regaining his children's trust—at least with *one* of his children.

"Do you want me to order it for you?" Rory asked. "I'll ask them to make sure it's not too hot."

"I can order," Belle said. "Fiona lets me."

"Okay!" Rory responded. She wanted to touch Seamus and be touched by him, but they both knew that any public sign they were more to each other than friends was a bad idea. Until the course was over. And then, how long could he remain in Sultan? His children needed to get back to school....

Behind her, she heard Lauren say, "Would you *please* just leave me alone? There's no one like me here who is my age. These are my friends."

"Friends to whom you've lied about something pretty basic."

With the espresso machine running, Rory doubted the group by the stove could hear them. She had to strain to do so.

"You're the one who's talking about moving here," Lauren accused. "And I like it, but you're picking on me. Why did you follow me?"

Rory stood to place her own coffee order and with her one good arm she managed to lift Belle to a stool at the counter so she could place hers.

"Because you're being untrustworthy. You're lying to other people right and left, which makes me think you've lied to me, as well."

"About what?"

"Why don't you collect your coffee and mine and we can return to the house to discuss it?"

"You never noticed a single thing I did until we came here."

"Let's talk about this at home."

Rory was fairly sure she knew what would happen—either on the way back to Empire Street or when they reached the house. Lauren would distract her father from her own behavior by raising the subject of her mother.

She had the same feeling she'd experienced during the avalanche; of being affected by forces beyond her control. She was seeing Seamus and she suspected that she was going to continue to become closer to him. But in doing so, she was entering into a complicated situation. He had four children and a different relationship with each child. When the SMS course ended, who would Rory be to those children? Their father's girlfriend? What would he expect of her in that role? What would they expect? And what could she expect of them?

Her father had thought Seamus wanted only a casual relationship with her. She knew already that he wanted something quite different. Her father had been wrong, wrong, wrong. What Seamus wanted was more challenging and also more important. Rory wondered if her father would think her competent to deal with *that* role—in essence, stepmother to four children whose mother had died suddenly and violently.

Wait, she told herself. *Let it play out. That's all you can do now.*

Rory sat at the counter with Belle and asked her what she'd done that day. They discussed Belle's stuffed animals, one of whom, Belle said, had caught a cold. Not Mouse, but Elsie Cow, who was now in bed and covered up.

Rory felt a hand on her shoulder—Seamus's.

Beside her, Lauren was paying for her own and her father's coffee. "I got mine for *here,*" she said. "Yours is *to go.*"

Leave, Dad. Leave.

"Want to go for a walk with Belle and me?" Seamus asked, as Rory paid for her coffee and stuffed a dollar in the tip jar.

I'm no longer working with him. Had her father shifted her to office work so that would be the case? Why would he facilitate her being with Seamus, if he believed Seamus would lead her on and then leave Sultan?

She shrugged. "I guess so. I'm struggling a little with how it looks. Because I work for the school."

Seamus smiled. "We have only a matter of a few days left at the school. I think you should stop worrying about that."

They stepped out into the spring day. Sultan was still a long way from summer, when there would be crowds of tourists, but a couple of the more vital stores had reopened.

Belle stopped often to sip her hot chocolate, and Rory and Seamus waited for her. Finally, they sat down on a bench outside the town toy store.

Belle exclaimed, "Stuffies!" and Seamus caught her hot chocolate cup as she dashed to the window to examine the array of stuffed animals. She spun around. "Daddy, can I get a new stuffy?"

Seamus looked thoughtfully at his youngest. He realized he couldn't remember buying her a single stuffed animal in her life. He couldn't remember what he'd ever bought for her birthday or Christmas. He *had* bought presents—he'd asked Fiona what he should get. Now he said, "Yes."

"Can Rory get one, too, so we can play?"

"I have some, Belle," Rory said quickly. "They're at my grandmother's house."

"At Miss Sondra's?"

Rory laughed at this name for her grandmother. "Yes."

"I bet you could use another one," Seamus said. Then, more softly, "I want to give you something. Many things."

"You really don't have to."

"Which one do you like?" Belle asked. "Can we go in?"

"After you finish your hot chocolate," Seamus told her. He turned to Rory. "You know, I think I should get something for each of them. A souvenir of being here and completing the course."

Souvenirs were not something you collected from the place where you lived. A memento of being somewhere, Rory thought, had to do with leaving.

With his returning to Telluride.

She had assumed too much. Far too much. His gift for her might be farewell.

No.

She forced her mind back to what Seamus had said. "I think that's a really good idea."

"I'd like to buy Beau a pair of skis from that shop where he works. Surely they'll give me a discount, with all the work he's done there."

"A big discount," Rory agreed. "Look into it."

"I don't want this to be a long-distance relationship," he said.

Rory blinked at the non sequitur. Either he was a mind reader or the thing foremost in her mind was also first in his. "You're going back to Telluride," she said, as lightly as possible.

"I'd like you to come, too."

CHAPTER TEN

HE'D BEEN AT THE HOUSE for an hour, waiting for Lauren, while Rory and Belle played with stuffed animals in Belle's room. The warthog that Seamus had bought Rory was bossing around Mouse, Elsie Cow and Belle's new squid, Squish.

Finally, Lauren came home.

Seamus nodded toward Belle's room, so that Lauren would know they weren't alone. "Shall we go upstairs to talk?"

Lauren gave him a wary look, and he thought how pretty she was and how much she looked like Janine. A spark went through him as he remembered Janine's laughter, her silly streak, vibrancy in the midst of her usual anger and fear. "Yesss," Lauren said with effort, drawing out the word.

Still wearing her parka, she followed him up the stairs and down the hall to an unoccupied bedroom with its single bed, its vanity table and two chairs by the filmy curtains. Seamus walked to one of the chairs and sat down.

Lauren sat on the bed, beside the door, ready to flee.

He'd done little in the past hour but think— about Rory and the possibility of her living with them in Telluride, but mostly about what he had to say to Lauren and the rules and restrictions he needed to impose. He worried that rules would make her wilder; that if he restricted her, she would make foolish choices just to thwart him.

"Here are the rules," he said. "You've made friends in Sultan. I think your friends are too old for you and that the males may want more than friendship from you. You're fourteen years old and you need someone to talk intelligently to you about boys, but I'm not sure it can be me."

"It's never been you. For anything. You didn't even know when I got my first period." Her voice accused. "Fiona's the only one who has ever told me anything. At least she's open-minded for someone her age. But I guess she's not coming back."

"She won't be with us as often as she used

to be. Her family needs her, which wasn't the case earlier." He refocused. "The first rule: You can see your friends at the coffeehouse, the ski area or here. When you're going out, you tell me where you're going and when you'll be back. I don't want you going to their houses."

"Things are *different* here. Kids of all ages hang out together. They just like to ski. They're not druggies or anything."

"Did you hear me?"

She rolled her eyes. "Yes. I don't care. We'll only be here a few more days."

"The next rule: Don't lie to me. Period. If you lie to me, you will be grounded."

She looked away, toward the doorway, already gone.

"Those are the rules for right now. Please follow them."

"Mom used to make rules," she said.

A cloud lifted and Seamus suddenly saw Janine before him, gazing straight into the eyes of Lauren—or Beau—saying, "Hear this: Don't lie to me. Ever."

Like him.

Peace came softly, briefly.

"She made good rules," Seamus said.

Lauren stole a look at him. Her wide mouth turned down as she faced the floor.

"Lauren."

She looked up.

"How would you feel about Rory coming to Telluride with us?"

Lauren shrugged. "I figured you'd do that."

He wasn't sure what she meant. And right now he was afraid to ask.

RORY LAY IN her double bed in the pink house, where she'd lived for so many years. She counted. Five... Six, at least...

What was she going to do?

Seamus had asked her to go to Telluride, where she had no employment. And that would mean yet *another* job change on her résumé. She was supposed to choose between working with her father—and perhaps moving into a position of more responsibility at the Sultan Mountain School—or being with Seamus.

Logic told her what to do. Intuition seconded it. Sultan was her home. And she could not abandon another job after just a few months at it. But could she make Seamus understand?

She hugged the warthog that Belle had insisted she get. Rory had named it Mrs. Turpin and explained to Belle and Seamus that it came from a story she'd read in which one of the characters had been called a warthog.

Finally, she reached for the cordless phone beside her bed and dialed the Empire Street house. Seamus answered.

"It's Rory."

"Hi. I was just thinking about you—again."

"I can't…go with you. I can still see you when I have free time. I can come to Telluride for a day or two sometimes—I'd like that. But my work is here. I need to honor the commitment I've made."

"For your father."

"For *me*. My résumé shows me hopping from one job to another. I'm actually perfect for the work I'm doing now, and I want to keep doing it. I would feel…flaky…if I went with you."

A pause. "I understand. I'm disappointed, but that's the way it is."

Sultan and Telluride were little more than an hour apart. An hour and fifteen or twenty minutes, say.

"And evenings," Rory said. "It's not that far."

"On the other hand, you're going to be out of a place to live soon."

"Yes, I know. But I'm always welcome at my grandmother's. I won't be homeless."

"You could live in Telluride and commute," Seamus suggested.

"The weather is too unpredictable. The passes close in bad weather, and then I wouldn't be able to get to work. Seamus, I *want* to be closer to you. I just know it's wrong not to fulfill my duty here. I need to be here, and I'm *sorry.* I know you can't just pick up and move your business…"

"Oh, I've thought about it." Standing in the living room of the Victorian where he and his children had been living for the past several months, he considered it again.

The plan had seemed perfect. Settle in Sultan. Move his employees to Sultan or let them commute. Even have two studios—one in Telluride, one in Sultan. And it was time for him to get his mind on Ki-Rin, the dragon boy who was his creation and his family's means of support. He wanted Rory to see his life in Telluride, to be part of that life. He wanted to be tied to her.

And that was the answer.

Standing in the living room, holding the phone, watching Caleb play with a tilting maze that had been his choice as a souvenir, he knew simply that he must find a way to join his life to Rory's, and she must join hers to his.

Lauren and Beau were upstairs watching a movie and Belle was asleep.

He said, "Can I come over?"

"Yes."

THEY LAY TOGETHER, dressed, on her Victorian four-poster, Mrs. Turpin sitting on the pillows against the headboard.

Seamus kissed her as he'd wanted to since they parted that morning. He wrapped his fingers in her hair and brushed his lips to her lush eyebrows and across the freckles on her nose. He found her mouth and touched his lips to hers, each kiss falling upon the one before. He said, "Will you marry me?"

Rory grew perfectly still. The room around her seemed cavernous, dark, magical. *Will you marry me?*

She had been asked once before, by a boy she'd thought of as selfish and immature.

This was entirely different.

He was so sure. But was she sure, as well?

"I still couldn't live in Telluride," she said at last.

"Yes, but we'd be united. I want that with you—I want you to be part of my family."

The prospect terrified her, and she couldn't have said why. At the same time, it seemed like her destiny, as if Seamus and his kin were made for her and she for them.

"I will," she said. "But maybe not right away? I think I'm a little afraid."

He kissed her again. "Thank you." Another kiss. "Thank you."

"TOMORROW'S YOUR DAY OFF," her father said to Rory on the Lees' last day in Sultan. "What are you going to do?"

She and Seamus had told no one of their engagement. Seamus planned to tell his children today, and Rory had not offered to be there. If the children objected to her, she wanted them to have the freedom to say so to Seamus privately.

Rory did, however, want to tell her father,

her grandmother and Samantha, and she would do that today.

The first person was the hardest one to inform....

"I'm going to drive to Telluride, just for the day."

Her father gazed at her, his eyes direct, unyielding. "You remember what I said."

"Actually," she interrupted, "we're going to spend the day finding an engagement ring."

Kurt Gorenzi sat down. He touched the arms of his chair. He looked up and smiled. "Well, good. I like that. That's actually great."

Rory could see that he meant it.

"But I'll hate to lose you," he said. "Here, I mean."

Yes, Rory thought, no use pretending you hate to give me away like a traditional father, you hate for your daughter to leave the home where she was raised, all your protection, everything you never gave me. She dismissed the bitter thoughts.

"You won't be losing me. I'm going to continue living in Sultan, maybe with Grandma. I told Seamus that I need to honor my commitment to this job. I'm proud of what I'm

doing here, and I don't want to leave. So…
we're going to be together sometimes and
apart sometimes."

Her father nodded, thinking it over. Again,
he smiled his crusty smile. "You've turned
out fine, Rory," he said.

SONDRA SAID, "YES, I'm happy for you, Rory.
Just don't rush. You don't know what marriage is. It will be the hardest thing you've
ever done, no matter how much you love
him."

Her grandmother had been a widow for de-
cades and had never remarried, although she
certainly could have, Rory reflected. Sondra
Nichols was beautiful still.

"You have freedom now," the older woman
continued. "That's something you can't buy.
When you marry, it's gone. I'm not saying
there aren't positive aspects to marriage. I'm
just telling you to be sure."

"I'm sure," Rory said. "And I've told him I
want to hold off on the ceremony for a little
while. To be absolutely sure."

Her grandmother embraced her. They
stood beside the bed in the room that had

been Rory's growing up. Her grandmother was pleased to have her back.

Sondra said, "So many changes for you, Rory. Desert's moving away. Her house being sold. Working for your father. But you do seem happy."

"I am."

"And I think it's better," Sondra said, "easier for you, that is, that the mother of those poor children is dead, rather than simply divorced from their father. Well, easier in some ways and harder in others."

"She'll always be their mother," Rory said.

"I'm not being callous, dear, and I understand that their grief will never completely heal. I just mean that the last thing you need, in taking on a husband and four children, is some kind of rival for the affection of those children. Or for his, for that matter."

Rory nodded, not wanting to hear any more of this advice. Janine was dead, and absolutely Rory would not have had her dead. If Janine had lived and remained married to Seamus, Rory doubted that Seamus would ever have fallen in love with her or she with him.

"I've been insensitive to say these things,"

Sondra told her. "I just know that everything that happened when your mother died had been set in motion from the time she met your father."

Rory sat on her bed. She lifted her face to see the older woman's. The death of her daughter had been the most painful loss in Sondra Nichols's life, and Rory knew that.

"I think the way your father was with her," Sondra said, "is something like he has been with you. Distant, uninvolved. He's a man's man."

"He can talk just fine," Rory said. She knew she hadn't expressed what she wanted Sondra to know. "I mean, he knows how to say what he thinks and feels. He has talked to me a few times now, since I've been working for SMS, and he's told me some truly nice things."

"Yes, you've shared that with me," her grandmother replied. "And I'm glad, Rory. I don't believe that he's a bad man at all. I simply think he was emotionally inaccessible, where your mother was concerned. She needed to talk about her feelings, and he couldn't do that. He came from a different culture; the mining culture, if the truth be told."

Her father, too, Rory remembered, had mentioned that his background was quite different from her mother's. That had been an element of his warning about becoming involved with Seamus.

Remembering that, she shivered. What if she couldn't give Seamus what he needed in a mate? What if he needed someone better educated or more worldly? He might not realize that immediately. He might not see it until it was too late.

We won't marry right away. We'll have a long engagement, she reminded herself.

"Well, Seamus isn't emotionally inaccessible," she said at last. "Not with me, at any rate. And he's doing the best he can with the kids."

Her grandmother touched her cheek. "I love you, Rory darling," she said.

SEAMUS HAD DECIDED to tell his children together. He knew Rory thought they should each be encouraged to express their true feelings about the engagement. Perhaps he was a coward for telling them all together, where sibling approval might drown out any dissenters.

So they assembled in the living room of the Empire Street house, their belongings half packed for their departure. He'd asked them to sit down there; he'd said he had something to tell them.

"We're moving here," Lauren predicted, without enthusiasm. She'd seemed depressed ever since the conversation when Seamus had given her the new rules. But maybe the rules weren't the reason. He suspected that Jay Norris had wasted no time in spreading the word that Lauren was fourteen years old.

All four children sat on the couch, with Seuss at Beau's feet, and Seamus drew up a chair across from them. "Rory and I are engaged to be married."

There was no instantaneous reaction, either of pleasure or displeasure.

Belle's eyebrows drew together slightly. "She'll be our mom?"

"*Step*mom," said Lauren, with less sensitivity than she usually showed her little sister. "Like in *Cinderella*."

Thank you, Lauren, Seamus thought.

Belle said, "Rory's not mean."

Caleb said, "Is that all? Can I go outside?"

Seamus considered his younger son. "You don't have anything you want to say?"

"I like Rory," he said and shrugged. Uncomplicated. The easiest of Seamus's children, which often made Seamus wonder if Caleb would somehow slip through the cracks, simply because he didn't *demand* attention by acting out or behaving as a loner.

"Yes, you can go outside. If you're using your snowskate, wear your helmet."

Caleb nodded resignedly, pushed off the couch and stood.

Beau stood, too, without asking. "I'm going to walk Seuss."

"Beau?" Seamus looked up at him, waiting for Beau to meet his eyes. "Anything *you* want to say?"

Beau shook his head.

And gave Seamus not a clue to his feelings, but simply picked up Seuss's leash and said, "Here, boy."

"You don't want to hear what *I* have to say," challenged Lauren.

"That may be, but I'd prefer you to say it, anyway," Seamus answered, almost without thinking.

She snorted. "I don't think it *matters* what any of us think or say or want, anyhow. All that matters is what *you* want."

Seamus didn't know how to respond to this. Was it true? Of course it mattered what his children wanted. But would their feelings change his decision to marry Rory? Absolutely not.

"You're probably going to want to move here to be with her and there's *nothing* in this town, and the school's not that good," Lauren continued.

"I got the impression you wanted to live here."

Lauren shrugged.

"You like going to fire-juggling classes with Rory, don't you?"

"That doesn't mean I want you to *marry* her."

"I've never thought it did mean that."

Belle said, "I want Rory to be my mom."

"Well, speak for yourself," snapped Lauren.

"She just did," Seamus pointed out. He smiled at Belle and asked her, "Where's Squish?"

"He's playing with Mouse. He wants to

come out here, though," Belle said, and she ran toward her room to get her toys.

"So is she moving to Telluride or are we moving here?" Lauren asked gloomily.

"Neither, at the moment. She doesn't want to leave her job here, and I can't pack up the studio in a moment. Also, I need to get back to work."

Lauren shrugged and sat down on the floor to play with Belle.

CHAPTER ELEVEN

FIONA AWAITED THEM in Telluride, and Belle, in particular, greeted her happily. Rory had followed the Lees in her own car; the splint allowed her to grasp the steering wheel with her left hand as well as her fully functional right. She planned to return to Sultan later on in the day. Not only did she have to work the next morning, but both she and Samantha had to move out of Desert's house, and then clean the Victorian.

Still, Rory had promised to come to Telluride, to visit Seamus's studio and to shop with him for an engagement ring.

His house was large, built in Victorian style and painted pale yellow with white trim. However, despite the vintage exterior, the house was actually modern. Seamus and Janine had been the first owners. Now, as Seamus and Rory walked under oaks much older than the structure, Seamus said, "First, let me show you the house. Then, we'll drive into town."

They entered through the mudroom. Even after Janine's death the family had continued to use this back door as their main entrance to the house. Seeing the laundry hampers and the washer and dryer, Rory remembered vividly what Seamus had told her.

He led her through the kitchen and into a dining room with Spode china on the walls and in the china cabinet, then on to the living room, which was furnished with antiques. What struck Rory at once was that the house appeared to have been decorated professionally. It wasn't like a home where people actually lived, but more like a vacation home for someone wealthy.

"It's very clean," she said.

"Maid service," Seamus explained.

Fiona had greeted Rory cordially, and now she trailed after Seamus and Rory as they explored the house. He led her up the stairway, over luxuriously springy carpeting, to the children's rooms, each with a separate bath. Fiona's room was downstairs, behind the kitchen, and Fiona showed Rory that herself. Books covered one wall, and there was also a small television, DVD player and VCR. Fiona's interest in opera and ballet showed in her selection of tapes and DVDs. Above the stereo was an extensive CD collection.

"This house is so…opulent," Rory finally said to the older woman.

"It's not what I was used to," Fiona answered. "But he does pretty well for a man alone—existing, I mean."

"The children need him," Rory said simply.

Fiona was quiet. Finally, she said, "Yes."

She was a cipher, this woman. Rory suspected she'd led an interesting life, yet the two of them had scarcely had a chance to talk. Seamus had told Fiona of the engagement over the phone. Now that she was alone with Fiona, Rory wanted to draw her out, to find out who she was. "Seamus says you're invaluable to him and the children. He said you did all the right things for the kids—and with them—when Janine died."

"As much as anyone could." Fiona shook her head and said, "She should never have bought a gun."

"You don't say that to the children," Rory guessed.

"I have. Lauren doesn't want to hear it. For her, her mother can do no wrong, and maybe that's as it should be." Fiona gazed out the nearest window. Her face was lined from many seasons in the mountains, in the high country under the sun. Against it, her hair was unusually thick, white and gray.

"How did you meet the Lees?" Rory asked.

"I knew Janine. We'd run into each other professionally."

Rory waited, eyeing Fiona curiously.

"I'm a judge," Fiona said. "Retired."

How had Seamus never once mentioned this?

Abruptly, Rory felt her own lack of education. She said, "That must have been really difficult. I doubt there were many women attorneys when you…started."

"You're right about that. But it's all in how you look at things. Almost any disadvantage can be turned to an advantage."

This woman was a good role model, Rory thought. Seamus was lucky to have her as part of his household.

"Well, when I retired, and Janine said she could use some help with the kids, I thought, 'Why not?' Neither of my children had children, then—they do now, which is why I want to spend more time with them."

"Seamus said something about their needing you." Rory said this anxiously. Suddenly, she did not want this woman to leave the Lee household. Rory sensed she had done more than could be expressed to hold all the Lees together.

"Well, yes. Some. But Telluride's my home. And Seamus has made clear that I always have a place with this family. Which is nice. I do own a house, but in the past few years I've rented it out."

If she owned property in Telluride, she was a wealthy woman, Rory reflected.

"It's good for him," Fiona said, "that he found you. Some men are better off alone, but he's not one of them. He was made for marriage. I'm not sure Janine was, but it's always more difficult for women."

"How so?" Rory asked.

"Well, there are traditional expectations associated with being a wife. And I'm not saying that a woman should necessarily fulfill all those expectations. But now there is also an expectation that she have a career. And be a good mother. And mothering's different from when I did it. Janine seemed to need all kinds of things that..." Fiona shrugged. "An intercom from the baby's room. A *separate* room for a baby. Now, after a certain age I say, yes, why not? But my husband and I always tucked ours into bed between us."

"You weren't afraid of rolling over on them?"

"No." Fiona laughed. "Not at all. And I'm not trying to give you a bad idea of Janine. She was a strong woman, but she put a lot of pressure on herself. She did far more than she needed to."

They heard footsteps in the hall, and both glanced up. Seamus stood in the doorway, his coat on. "Ready to find that ring?"

"Yes," Rory said. Impulsively, she touched Fiona's arm. "Thank you for visiting with me."

Fiona smiled. "Belle thinks she should be allowed to go on the hunt for the ring."

"So she has told me," Seamus said. "But she was really quite good when I told her that we prefer to go alone."

"Do we?" Rory asked. "As far as I'm concerned, they're all welcome to join us. You, too, Fiona."

Seamus seemed to consider this. "Okay. I'll tell them. I imagine Beau will turn us down in favor of a reunion with his computer. And Lauren's already sending e-mails to all her friends. To whom, incidentally, she sent text messages from Sultan at five dollars a day. That's fifty text messages a day."

"You might need to look into a different cell-phone plan," Rory said, "if she's going to keep doing that."

Seamus smiled. "Let me see what the kids say."

IN THE END, only Lauren stayed at home, with Seuss. Seamus drove the rest of them, including Fiona, in the Toyota SUV hybrid. Beau and Caleb both brought their iPods and earphones and listened to music the whole way into town.

Telluride was a metropolis, compared to Sultan. Beau and Caleb counted five galleries and three jewelry stores where Seamus and Rory might find a suitable engagement ring. Caleb was stopped on the sidewalk several times by school friends he hadn't seen for months. Beau nodded to a few classmates, but none of his came over to speak.

They all entered the first gallery, where Belle hurriedly pressed her nose to a glass case, trying to see rings.

The rings were beautiful. "I guess," Rory said, "that we need to find a set."

"I don't see why," Seamus told her. "We can get rings that match to a certain degree, but if you want just one ring for both engagement and marriage, that's fine with me."

Rory liked large pieces. She preferred silver or white gold, rather than yellow gold. She tried on several rings, rings constructed of precious metals by artisans and set with precious stones. The boys suggested the largest and most unusual ones in the gallery for her to try, and she tried them, and then they all moved on to the next store.

An hour later, Beau and Caleb were getting restless and Belle had begun asking for hot chocolate, when Seamus called Rory to a display case in the Oak Street Gallery of Fine Arts. "What do you think of this one?"

It was made of both white and yellow gold, shaped into flames, surrounding a swirling cauldron of gems, a diamond, two emeralds, a citrine and a sapphire. The ring was unusually earthy, and its theme was fire. It was exquisite. "There are five stones," she said.

"It's elemental," Seamus remarked.

"One for each of you," Rory said, looking up into his face.

His eyes nearly glowed as he gazed down at her. "Do you want to try it?"

"Yes!"

It was lovely on her hand—and it fit on her ring finger. Seamus paid, and Rory wore it from the store.

Belle said, "You have it because you're a fire princess."

"Thank you, Belle."

They stopped at a coffeehouse, then, so that Belle could have her hot chocolate and the rest of them could order drinks, as well.

Seamus said, "Next stop is Ki-Rin Studio."

"Yes!" said Rory. Finally, she would get to see Seamus's work. She had seen Ki-Rin before—movie posters, DVD covers. But she'd never watched one of the films. Also, she wanted to know what went into running an anime studio.

"And Rory will get to meet Elizabeth," said Beau.

Seamus shot him a look.

Rory lifted her eyebrows.

Fiona laughed silently.

"Who is Elizabeth?" Rory asked.

"The last girlfriend Dad *didn't* marry," Beau said.

Seamus said, "Actually, she has been managing the studio in my absence. She's one of my artists."

Rory smiled. "I look forward to meeting her."

"She doesn't like pets, and she didn't like to take us anywhere," Caleb said. "She wasn't very nice."

"She hasn't met Seuss," said Beau.

"We should let him jump on her with muddy paws," Caleb suggested.

Seamus ignored the bantering and took Rory's hand. He slid her ring off and then back on, and after that he kissed her.

ELIZABETH HAD RAVEN hair, angular features that would have suited a model, blue eyes and a tall, strong body. Her black hair hung just below her shoulders, and she had long, straight bangs. Seamus had already told her that he was engaged, before he returned to Telluride.

Now, in the foyer of the glass-fronted Victorian building that housed Ki-Rin Studio, she held out her hand to Rory and smiled beautifully. She was a gorgeous woman. "Congratulations," she said.

Fiona told her, "You congratulate the man and give the bride your best wishes."

"Best wishes," Elizabeth echoed with a shrug. "I'm pleased to meet you, Rory. Are you an artist, too?"

"She's a fire dancer," Beau said. "We got a dog. His name's Seuss. He's a German shepherd. They shed a lot."

Rory wanted to burst out laughing.

Elizabeth gave a small shudder. "I'm glad he's yours," she said politely.

"So am I," Beau said.

"A fire dancer," Elizabeth remarked. "Wow. Well, come in and see the studio."

She and Seamus led the group on a tour past the drawing tables, where they met Seamus's other employees. Elizabeth showed them the computers and film equipment. One wall of the studio was painted with a mural of Ki-Rin, in the process of transforming from boy to dragon.

"Dad made Ki-Rin for me," Beau said. "I'm Ki-Rin."

"I'm Jiro," Caleb announced. "He's another dragon, but he's *all* dragon. He teaches Ki-Rin."

"Do you have characters inspired by Lauren and Belle?" Rory asked Seamus, remembering him saying that all the children had characters in Ki-Rin's world.

"Koneko and Cho," Caleb told her. "Koneko's evil. She's Lauren's character. That's what she wanted. She said, 'I want to be someone bad.' Koneko's *really* bad. Cho's Ki-Rin's little sister, and she's all girl, not part dragon or anything."

Rory was enchanted.

Elizabeth handed her a small book, like a graphic novel, its pages in color. "That's the first volume. Take it. It's in English, but it reads from back to front."

"Wow." Rory couldn't stop smiling. *I'm blessed.*

Fiona said, "They're very earthy stories. The characters are connected to the land, to specific places. Magical springs, caves."

Elizabeth hunted out other volumes. "Not all of these are in color, but let's get you a full set. Let me find a box."

Elizabeth, Rory thought, was nice. Rory followed her toward a closet in the back of the room.

Glancing back at Rory, Elizabeth said, "You can have him. I mean, don't take that the wrong way. I just wasn't interested in being the kids' caretaker. He's a great boss. But it was always like he never had any time for his kids himself." She lowered her voice to a whisper. "They hardly ever came here, because if they did, he'd always take off." Speaking normally again, she said, "No hard feelings, eh?"

Rory shook her head, smiling. "None."

RORY WANTED TO see Lauren before she drove back to Sultan. Seamus had said that Lauren had been less than enthusiastic about their engagement.

When they returned to the house, Rory climbed the stairs, went alone to the door of Lauren's bedroom and knocked.

A moment. Another moment. Feet on the floor. Crossing the expensive carpet.

The door opened.

Lauren said, "Oh, hi."

She wore pink capri tights and a pale blue

crop top. Her blond hair was in a ponytail on top of her head.

"I just wanted to say goodbye before I head back to Sultan."

Lauren nodded and turned away from the door, an invitation to enter her room.

Rory came inside and looked around, trying to know the girl by what she saw on her walls. The walls themselves were pale yellow, and Lauren had hung framed prints on them. All were of women athletes. A female baseball player at bat. Mia Hamm. A female boxer. A female hockey player. On a white desk sat a framed eight-by-ten. Rory stepped closer to see the subject, a blond woman in a Fair Isles sweater, sunglasses pushed back in her hair. She radiated tremendous vibrancy and strength in the photograph, as though she was ready to schuss down a mountain or descend a rocky trail on a mountain bike at breakneck speed. Unlike Rory's mother, who'd been petite, Janine had been tall, broad-shouldered and obviously strong. Janine had been beautiful, without model-perfect beauty but with the sort of healthy good looks that come from taking excellent care of one's self. Clearly, she was an athlete.

And missing from her eyes was the vulnerability that showed in Rory's photos of Kristen Gorenzi.

"Your mother was beautiful," Rory said.

"She never put up with anything from anyone," Lauren said. "She wouldn't want me to just let Dad push me around."

"You think your dad's pushing you around?"

"Yes. And, like, he hasn't even been there for any of us, not until we came to Sultan. But now he wants to make rules. He doesn't realize he can't just appear and expect us all to bow and worship."

Rory suppressed a smile. "He was worried in Sultan. *I* was kind of worried, too, Lauren."

Lauren frowned. She sank onto her bed. "It's not going to work, you know."

A chill passed through Rory. "What?"

"You marrying my dad and then we're a happy family. You haven't been here. You don't know what it's like, and you don't know how it *used* to be."

Rory said carefully, "I'm sorry you believe that. You're right that I don't know what your family life was like before I met any of you."

"Or when Mom was here. She took care of me, and she taught me to take care of myself. I was only ten when she died, but she'd already taught me some aikido and how to load and shoot a gun. And it's good she did, because once she was gone there was no one else."

"What about Fiona?"

Lauren shrugged. "She isn't my mom."

And her dad, Rory knew, had disappeared, distanced himself from his children's lives. She said, "Lauren, I'm not trying to do anything like that." To turn Seamus's family into one big, happy family? Of course, she was. Of course, she had been trying to since she'd met him. Who was she kidding? "I guess that's not true," she admitted. "But Lauren, I didn't just agree to marry your dad because I'm in love with him. I love all of you, too. You don't have to love me back, but that's the way it is."

"I used to think of you like a *friend,*" Lauren said. "But you were just after my dad."

"I just told you that's not true," Rory said, surprised by Lauren's take on things. "I loved teaching you staff-twirling and belly dance.

I loved snowboarding with you and hanging with you, in general."

"But *we* need him. We need him, and you don't. You've got a dad."

Rory wished she could make Lauren appreciate the irony—*ironies*—of that remark. She also wished… "I wish you saw this as getting something extra, instead of losing something valuable. It's absolutely not my intention to take your dad away from you. In fact, it's rather the reverse."

"But you're not my mom. And you're only, like, fifteen years older than me. No way am I going to call you Mom."

"I wouldn't ask that of you. Your dad wouldn't ask it of you, either."

"Why don't you just back off, knowing *I* don't want you to do this?" Lauren said.

Rory considered this. Lauren didn't want Rory to marry her father and she expected Rory to react to all that emotion and not marry him. And Rory knew perfectly well that if she made some sort of deal with Lauren—say, that she wouldn't marry Seamus *until* Lauren was okay with the arrangement—she could wait a lifetime before Lauren yielded.

Rory said, "I hear what you're saying. I'm not saying it makes a difference, but I *do* hear you, Lauren. The last thing I want is for you to hate me or believe I'm trying to take your dad from you."

"I don't think you're trying to take him from us. I just think that with you in the picture he has less to give us, that's all. And we already get little enough from him."

"I'm going to think about all these things," Rory said, "but I hope you'll still think of me as your friend. In any case, Lauren."

BACK AT HER grandmother's house in Sultan, Rory thought about Seamus and his family in Telluride, about Lauren's attitude, about Elizabeth, the studio manager, and about Ki-Rin. She'd brought the manga books home and had read part of the first one after a brief belly dance practice with Samantha, who had moved into one of the rooms at the hot springs. They had practiced in Rory's grandmother's living room, which was really too crowded for the enterprise. Clearly, they needed to find a new place to practice with fire, and that was going to be far more difficult than finding somewhere simply to belly dance.

Rory was getting ready for bed when Seamus called. "Mark your calendar for April third," he said.

"What is April third?"

"Lauren's birthday."

Rory's own was on the tenth. Rory had exchanged this information with Seamus on the night they'd spent together in the ski hut. His was November tenth. "When are the other kids' birthdays?"

"Caleb's is June fourth, Beau's, September fourth, and Belle's, July fifth."

"What are you getting Lauren?" Rory asked, groping for a pen on her bedside table, to make note of the children's birthdays. "And what are you going to do for her that day?" For her Sultan souvenir, Lauren had chosen a Sultan Mountain School jacket made of pile.

"I was hoping for your input."

"Actually, I'd like to choose a gift for her myself," Rory said. She would present Lauren with belly dance treasures selected from her own collection. Maybe... Her imagination went wild. Giving Lauren a coin bra, for instance, would affirm Lauren's maturity. And tribal belly dance costumes were beautiful.

"I know that," Seamus said.

"Seamus, she wants something from *you*. Something special that *you* choose."

Rory told him about her conversation with Lauren before leaving Telluride. She admitted, "It makes me want to say, 'Okay, we won't get married until you're happy with the idea.' But that's crazy. I just never expected this, and I suppose I should have. I thought she liked me—and she does like me. But she considered me a friend, and she sees this as a betrayal."

"She'll get beyond it," Seamus said.

"I don't know. It seems related to her loyalty to her mother, which is understandable."

"You think so?" Seamus said. "To be perfectly honest, lately I don't understand Lauren at all."

WHEN HE'D HUNG UP, Seamus considered everything that Rory had said and thought about her anxiety over Lauren's attitude.

Something for Lauren. For her birthday.

The seed of an idea had been planted in

the studio, when Beau had said, *Koneko's evil. She's Lauren's character. That's what she wanted. She said, 'I want to be someone bad.' Koneko's really bad.*

Yes, years ago, Lauren had told him that she wanted her Ki-Rin character to be evil.

And he had obliged. Koneko was a demoness who wished to kill the dragon boy Ki-Rin, in order to have the power of the sacred nature sites he protected. But *why* was Koneko as she was, tough and angry, unwilling to be intimidated by a dragon or anyone or anything else? *Janine. Lauren.* Did Koneko somehow embody the two of them?

But *why,* why was Koneko evil?

He considered his desire to make a character for Rory; in some ways, that character was already formed. But he needed to set aside his plans for the fire goddess.

Koneko, Koneko, Koneko… Something entirely Lauren's.

He knew now what he would give Lauren for her birthday. He would take her shopping, choose a gift *with* her, something she could keep forever. Jewelry, perhaps. But that would not be her main gift, the gift that might not be finished for two years.

Koneko needed her own story, her own movie. Already, Seamus knew her to be a likable villain. Ki-Rin's audience sympathized with Koneko, and it was unclear why, except that perhaps through the medium her insecurity came across. This story must explain her. As his mind wrapped around various possibilities, he also turned back to the question of why Janine was as she had been. What had formed her into someone so...

Frightened.

CHAPTER TWELVE

WHAT HAD FORMED Koneko?

What had formed Janine?

What was Lauren becoming?

These ideas whirled in Seamus's head. He wanted to work, yet in the past his studio had been the place he escaped to. Now, he wanted to work in the house—in the house where Janine had died, in the house where his children slept, and lived, and used their computers. Yes, the idea of moving to Sultan had been tempting. But he needed to clean house here, first. Or make his peace with this place. Or understand what was here and what lay beneath it.

Rory had given him the courage to begin.

Maybe if he understood Janine, he would not hate her anymore.

She *must* have been the way she was for a reason. The next morning, he called Rory on her cell phone and caught her working at the school office. He said, "I want to know why Janine was the way she was, and I'm wondering if she told women things she never told me. Will you ask your friend Samantha about anything Janine might have confided?"

Rory didn't answer at once. Then her low, almost boyish voice said, "You mean like an assault or something?"

"Anything."

"I don't think Samantha knows anything. She just told me that she suspected Janine had, I think she said, 'been through some stuff.' What was her family like?"

He heard a drawer slide open and then close.

"She was one of five sisters. A middle child. She used to talk to her sisters on the phone. Her parents are still both alive. They've come to visit the kids, but not often."

"What are they like?"

"Extremely academic. A very competitive family—the sisters competing for their parents' attention. You know. All her siblings have graduate degrees. One of them is a professor at Yale."

"Good grief." A hesitant, "You know I've never finished college. Barely started."

He did know that. She sounded unsure of herself—because she had no university degree?

Seamus had graduated from Cooper Union. What did it mean to him that Rory had never finished college? Was it a gap of some kind? He did feel a difference between them on that level. But Rory could do so many things he could not. She was a gifted dancer and performer, and she knew the backcountry around Sultan exceptionally well, perhaps almost as well as her father.

Well, *half* as well as her father, at least, which was saying a great deal.

He said, "I think you deserve an honorary degree in mountain terrain studies."

She laughed. "Maybe."

Now she sounded preoccupied. "Seamus, I don't think you're going to find any answers about Janine by digging into things you don't already know. If there's a dreadful family secret, how do you expect to learn it? Yes, if you ask me, she sounds like people I know who've been sexually assaulted—or maybe she had been in a battering situation. She was afraid. And it was probably critically important to her not to be hurt again."

Seamus considered. He said, "Can you talk now, or is this a bad time?"

"It's fine. I'm looking for something. I can listen at the same time."

So he told her about Koneko; that Koneko needed her own story.

Rory said, "That sounds like a great thing to do. For Lauren and for you."

"Yes." He didn't say that, to him, the character of Koneko represented some blend of Lauren and Janine, but he sensed that Rory already knew that; that she knew what the project would do for him.

"Yes?" Rory said to someone else, not into the phone. Then, "I've got to go. Talk to you later." And she hung up.

HIS KIDS WOULD RETURN to school in Telluride the following day. Even Belle to her preschool. Rather than going into the studio, Seamus would stay at home to begin outlining his project. He would do as much of the work on Koneko as he could from home; the home that was the root of so many of his own demons.

Koneko had been born human, Seamus decided. She had *chosen* to become a demoness.

Why? For power. Because in her family she was powerless. She was the youngest daughter.

Why not make her older? The first to be given away in marriage, perhaps? He considered the notion, swept into the world of his creation, Ki-Rin's world in greater depth. The story behind Koneko.

JAY NORRIS STOOD in the doorway of her office, and Rory was finally fully aware of the sounds from outside the office.

Someone saying, "They're on their way."

"Your dad's collapsed."

Rory rushed from the room without closing the drawer of the filing cabinet where she'd been working. Her father lay in his office, crumpled beside his desk. "I can sit up," he was saying.

Carrie said just as emphatically, "And you're *not* going to."

Rory came and knelt beside her father, unsure if she was welcome there, obscurely unsure if she ever had a right to be there. Her father was holding his left arm.

Heart attack. She was sure of it, without

knowing anything about her father's choles-terol level or any other details of his health.

Sirens pealed on the streets of Sultan, an unusual sound for the sleepy little town.

Rory sat beside her father, watching his face.

Then she felt his calloused hand close over hers.

She looked at him. "You're going to be all right, Dad." And she couldn't remember ever calling him that before.

"I know," he said.

SHE DROVE TO Montrose, pausing on the way to call Seamus on her cell phone. He asked if she wanted him to come to the hospital, and she said no—it was better that he give his children what they need.

From the hospital, she spoke with others on the phone. Her grandmother, Samantha and Carrie at the Sultan Mountain School.

Physicians came and talked to her, and then she sat with her father while the doctors spoke to them both. Her father had had a heart attack, which fortunately had not damaged the heart. Rory listened to all the reasons in favor of an emergency triple bypass.

He could have died skiing out to get me that night.

He must have been experiencing symptoms for some time, Rory thought; symptoms he had shared with no one.

Her father nodded his agreement to the surgery, which was scheduled for the following morning, and when the doctors finally left his room, replaced by a parade of nurses, he said, "Rory, I want you to direct the Sultan Mountain School."

"Now? I don't know enough!"

"You do, and you'll learn more. I've already talked about this with Carrie, and she has agreed to help you learn the ropes. We'd planned to do it more gradually, but, well, I want you to take over now."

"I'm not going back to Sultan until you're out of surgery and okay."

"Well, you're not staying here through my convalescence. That's where I need you— running the school."

"Carrie can run the school."

"Actually, she can't. She has to make several trips to Canada over the next few months to see her family. Her mother's ill. You two are facing a similar situation. And her family takes precedence, as indeed it should."

"Yes," Rory agreed uneasily.

The unspoken had, in fact, been spoken. Rory's family should take precedence, as well.

But Rory knew what running the Sultan Mountain School entailed. There would be no nights in Telluride with Seamus and his family. She simply could not afford to be that far from the school. Did she *want* to be director of the Sultan Mountain School? No question it was the best job there was for her; the best career opportunity she'd ever had.

Of course, she wanted to do it.

But she knew what an all-consuming job it was. A small part of her whispered that it was no job for a wife and mother. When would she have time for Seamus, let alone his kids? And Seamus's work was in Telluride.

"Will you do it?" her father asked. "Can I count on you, Rory?"

She remembered that she had envied Desert when Desert's father had needed her.

And now Kurt Gorenzi needed Rory.

"Yes," she said. "Yes."

But what was this going to do to her relationship with Seamus?

Surely she wouldn't have to choose between her future husband and family and her own father's need.

"You'll be coming back to work, won't you?" she asked anxiously. Then swiftly she also said, "I'm sorry. Don't think about that now. Just think about coming through surgery, and then we'll help you with your rehab from there."

"I'm going to take care of rehab right here, Rory. I'm going to stay in a rehab facility. As soon as you know I'm out of the woods, I want you to get back to the school and keep it going. Put your all into it, because I know your all is exceptionally good."

How was she going to explain this to Seamus over the phone? Would it be any easier in person?

Of course not.

She checked into a hotel for the night and called him before returning to the hospital to be with her father.

"Everything all right there?" she asked.

"Yes," he said. "We're all fine. Tell me about your father. How's he doing?"

She told Seamus about the scheduled surgery. Then she said, "He wants me to run the school in his absence. In fact, it sounds a bit like that's his long-range plan, too."

Silence followed, lasting a second too long. "Well, that's what you need to do," Seamus answered.

"I have a commitment to you—and the kids. I'm confused, but I know that he's asked me to do this and I've said that I would. I should have talked with you first."

"Just out of curiosity, what would have happened if I'd raised objections?"

The question startled her. She did not want to answer. "I...I have to do this."

"I know. It wasn't a fair question."

"It was. I'm *sorry* I didn't ask you."

But Seamus, listening at the other end of the phone, remembered Janine and other decisions that had been made without his input or his blessing. *This is different. It's reasonable for Rory to help her father. She wasn't going to leave her job, anyhow.*

He knew, as well as she did, what running the Sultan Mountain School meant. It meant being on hand for emergencies, and it did not mean sleeping an hour away. It meant being available to instructors and clients who were out in the wilderness, even out overnight.

His kids were just returning to school in Telluride and he couldn't—wouldn't—take them out again before the end of the year. Rory's decision seemed to be forcing his hand, forcing him to choose between Telluride and Sultan. Not yet, not immediately.

But eventually.

Why they should have to choose between two locations little more than an hour apart baffled him. But that was the choice suddenly set before him.

"You've agreed to help him until he's ready to return to work," Seamus clarified.

"Well. I started to ask, but it seemed like putting pressure on him. And it's the perfect job for me, Seamus. You know it is."

"Yes," he said quietly.

But he had signed up for something like this once before. And when Janine died, he'd vowed that if he ever married again, it would be to a woman who made decisions in conjunction with him. Not alone, and not decisions he'd have to live with.

Now wasn't the time to fight about it. Not now, while Kurt lay in the hospital, right before he went into a dangerous operation.

But they would have to talk about this before they married.

And he would need to be convinced that Rory *wasn't* going to make decisions alone, the way Janine had.

He said, "I'll be there in the morning for his surgery. I don't want you to sit through that alone."

"Thank you," Rory said. "But you should get back before the kids are out of school."

"Fiona is here. Still, I understand what you're saying."

"I guess I'll see you tomorrow, then," she said, sounding far away. And as uncertain as he now felt.

THE OPERATION WAS LONG; the wait, tedious. Rory wasn't worried that her father would not survive the surgery and she knew he would do what was necessary to take care of his health. He was disciplined, and the heart attack had snuck up on him after years of eating high-cholesterol food and seeming to be fine. Rory had no doubt that he would change his dietary habits.

What troubled her more was the unacknowledged distance between her and Seamus, a distance that seemed to have grown in just a couple of days. When she suggested that if he wanted to return to Telluride she could easily wait alone, he said, "Of course not. Why would I do that?"

"You seem to be in another world. I figured you had your mind on Koneko, which is fine. I want you to feel as though it's okay to work."

He shook his head. "I was thinking about something else entirely."

"What?"

He regarded her thoughtfully. "I wasn't going to bring it up now."

"What?" she repeated, sensing that she might not like the answer.

"We need to agree to make decisions together."

Rory blinked several times before realizing what he must be talking about. "You mean my decision to direct the Sultan Mountain School."

He gave a small noncommittal shrug. "Things like that."

This issue, Rory realized, would take some thinking through before she responded. It was tempting to tell Seamus that her career decisions would always be hers and not subject to veto by him. Sometimes, after all, decisions couldn't be made together; compromises weren't always possible. "What if we disagree?" she asked.

"Then we talk about it and try to come to a reasonable solution together."

"Shall we pretend that I haven't actually made the decision that I've made, so that we can go through the motions of discussing it?"

"We're going to have to discuss it, in any case," he said.

Rory knew he was right and she didn't argue with his assessment. "If you'd like me to choose a job closer to Telluride when my father's ready to go back to work, we should discuss that. But maybe we don't have to talk about something that's not going to be an issue."

"How would it not be an issue? If you direct SMS, you can't live in Telluride. I think we both realize that."

"But my father may come back and take over again."

"You've said it's his long-range plan to hand off the position to you."

"I didn't say it was *my* long-range plan," she answered. "I'm not Janine," she added, then immediately wished she hadn't.

Seamus gazed at her for a long time.

"What are you thinking?" she asked.

"That I don't think you're Janine, and that we still need to discuss things."

"Maybe we should start with where you plan to live once we're married," Rory said.

"With you," he answered. "That's where."

She relaxed slightly. "We can… We can call off the engagement, if you think that's better."

Seamus felt the hair rise on the back of his neck. "Do *you* think it's better?"

"I think we're already arguing." Then she said in a rush, "I didn't *want* him to ask me to do this. I tried to get him to say it was temporary. I mean, I *did* want him to need me—before he did. Now, the timing's all wrong, and you're misinterpreting my decision to help him."

"I'm not."

"Oh, I know you think I'm doing it because it's the right thing to do, to help my father when he's sick, but I think you also believe I'm doing it because I care more about his opinion than yours."

Her own words stunned her to silence.

Seamus said, "Maybe that's why you *think* you're doing it."

"I don't care more about his opinion than yours."

"He's the only parent you've ever known, and for most of your life he's had nothing to do with you. Now, he's approving of you. I can't imagine you want to give that up or risk it by doing something that will disappoint him."

"I *did* risk it when I got involved with you."

"How much of a risk was that? After all, if I end up moving to Sultan, Kurt's end will be accomplished."

Rory began to suspect that her not-very-sound sleep the night before was affecting her reasoning. Maybe Seamus hadn't slept well, either, and that explained his behavior.

Seamus paced the waiting room and picked up a magazine. Rory sipped from a cup of bad coffee.

Too fast—we got engaged too fast. We fell in love too fast.

And yet it still felt right to her, as if her destiny was to marry Seamus Lee.

I can do it all. I can run the Sultan Mountain School and mother his children.

But she saw the sacrifice for Seamus. He would have to make the decision to move to Sultan. And it wasn't fair to put such a pressure on him.

She looked at the ring on her hand. The fiery cauldron. Then she took it off, stood up and handed it to him.

"I made a mistake," she said. "Taking this job. I suppose I had a choice all the way through, but it forces a decision about where you're going to live. I don't want to start a life with you that way. Let's just back off. If things are meant to be between us, they will be. But now is the time to hold off."

Seamus gazed down at Rory's ring. She thought that in taking the job as head of the Sultan Mountain School, in doing what her father had asked of her, she was forcing him to move to Sultan.

And if she continued to run the Sultan Mountain School, there was no other answer.

The rift between them seemed to be growing, and Seamus asked himself, *What has happened to us? How has this happened?*

But perhaps it had happened when he, returning to Telluride, had asked her to marry him. She, after all, still held a job in Sultan. And then her father had become incapacitated and he wanted her to step in. But also, this was her chance at a career, whereas he'd known success for many years.

How important was this work to her, really, in the long run? He could see the difference between Rory's unilateral decision to support her father by agreeing to run the school and Janine's unilateral decision to buy a handgun. But if Rory's new position was a long-term thing…

He didn't want to take the ring she had just given him back. He felt that by accepting it, he was letting her slip away and that he might never again…

What? Possess her? She's not yours.

She had said, *If things are meant to be between us, they will be.*

Did he believe that? Or did he believe that they *made* things happen?

Above all, he felt hurt. She had seemed so casual, handing it back.

Could he have broken their engagement just as easily; said, *If it's meant to be it will be?*

No. He didn't want to let her go, even now.

They were alone in the waiting room, and he was glad of that. He asked, "Are you in love with me?"

"*Yes,*" she whispered. "And I want to marry you and live with you and your children, but this is the wrong way to begin."

"How did it become wrong for you to help your father?"

"I don't know," she said. "And it's not. But I can't promise you that I'll be willing or able to walk away from this job when he's fit again. What if I love it? What if I don't want to give it up? What if, because of my job, you move to Sultan and it turns out to be the wrong thing for the kids? It might not be the best place for Lauren, after all."

"Please wear this," he said, pressing the ring back into her hand. "As a pledge that we will make it work."

Rory hesitated. She no longer knew what was best. She *did* care about the opportunity her father had just given her. And she cared about Seamus and his children. She slowly said, "Would you please keep it for me, instead?"

CHAPTER THIRTEEN

HE TOOK TO CARRYING the ring with him, and then, so that he wouldn't lose it, to wearing it on his little finger.

"Why do you have Rory's ring?" Beau asked when he saw it, three days after Kurt Gorenzi's successful bypass. Rory was back in Sultan, busy running the mountain school, and Seamus had returned to Telluride to try to focus on the Koneko project.

Seamus did not want to lie to his son. Nor did he want to discuss his rift with Rory. He should be able to put his life back together better than it had been before the family had gone to Sultan. He was closer to his children and he felt less angry at Janine.

Yet Rory had agreed to marry him and then run away at the first sign of conflict. And it wasn't as simple as fear of conflict, either. She had been afraid of a wrong start.

Belatedly, he'd remembered how her parents' marriage had ended—her mother dying while out skiing with a lover.

No wonder she might be a bit afraid of marriage.

Finally, he said, "I think she has cold feet."

"What does that mean?" Beau said.

"That she's not sure she wants to marry me."

"Because of Lauren," Beau said with certainty.

"What? No, it has nothing to do with Lauren. Well, no more than anything or anyone else." Briefly, he told Beau about Rory running SMS for her father and her concerns that maybe Sultan wasn't the right place for their family.

"Because of Lauren," Beau repeated, this time with an edge of bitterness.

"What's because of me?" She peered through the doorway, eyebrows drawn together in preparation for a fight.

"That Rory's not going to marry Dad."

Lauren looked interested but not remotely sorry.

Again, Seamus explained the true situation.

"I don't want to live in Sultan," Lauren said. "I hated it there."

"Once everyone found out you weren't sixteen," Beau said.

"Enough," Seamus interjected.

He wondered if Lauren had truly "hated" Sultan, if she now hated the idea of living there, the idea of leaving Telluride and, most of all, the thought of her father marrying Rory Gorenzi.

"In any case," he said, "there's some chance we'll be moving there when summer comes."

"I'm not going," Lauren said. "Forget it." And she left the room.

Beau gave Seamus a *What did I tell you?* look.

COULD HE TAKE his children out of school in Telluride, where they'd grown up, and move to Sultan, Colorado, just because he wanted to marry a woman whose work was there? For the first time in months, Seamus remembered that initially he'd wanted to take the kids to Sultan in part to free them from the sense of entitlement they'd seemed to have as children raised in Telluride. Now, he saw how silly that idea had been.

He was a wealthy man. He'd allowed his children cell phones, computers, iPods, state-of-the-art skis and snowboards, all the things their contemporaries had. If they felt entitled, he, not Telluride, was to blame. And they would feel every bit as entitled in Sultan. *Or* they would feel resentful at being deprived of things they knew he was able to provide. When Lauren had become interested in Rory's staff-twirling and dance classes, he'd somehow felt that his daughter was on a better path. What Rory had been doing seemed more wholesome than the too-fast life of Telluride.

But then his daughter had told some college students that she was sixteen—and why those people chose to befriend a sixteen-year-old was nearly as mystifying to him as them wanting to pal around with a fourteen-year-old. His vision of Sultan had changed. It had become a minefield, and Lauren was running through it heedlessly. Telluride had looked safer, and so he'd retreated.

I'm not going. Forget it.

Yes, he could make Lauren go to Sultan.

And she could make all their lives miserable in return.

His daughter, however, would not decide whether or not he married Rory.

He still wanted to be with Rory; still wanted her for his wife. She was confused and afraid. He didn't think he was projecting that.

He would give her what she'd asked for—time.

He would go to Sultan to see her as often as he could without depriving the kids of the time they deserved, time he was now determined to give them. He would take another look at Sultan as a possible home for his children. And he would hope for a miracle where Lauren was concerned.

SEAMUS AND RORY talked on the phone most nights. On the evening of April second, a Friday, Rory said, "I got the day off tomorrow. Carrie is going to cover for me. Unless…did you want to do something alone with Lauren?"

"The two of us have something planned. Or actually I have something in mind that I'm going to spring on her. A father-daughter thing."

"That's what you should do, then."

"But will you join us for dinner? She's already asked to go to her favorite Thai restaurant, and we have reservations."

"Great. I want to bring her present to her."

"Rory, thank you for getting the day off. I wouldn't have asked."

Rory knew that he regretted what had happened the day of her father's surgery. She was sorry they'd argued, but she still believed a situation that required them to live in a particular place because of her job was not a good situation. His job, yes. But even directing the Sultan Mountain School... She'd been happy just being an instructor. Responsibility for the whole school was overwhelming. Already she worried that she might have to fire an employee.

She'd talked to her father on the phone, of course, explaining the situation, which so far only involved rumors—but the rumors were serious. She'd asked the instructor if there was any truth to the gossip that he'd shared a joint with a client on a backcountry overnight trip. And she hated being in this position, and with a man who was roughly her same age. He'd denied it, but she'd still had to say, "Because if that happens, we'll let you go. You know that."

Then there were all the small rules that had to be followed precisely for insurance reasons, and her part in enforcing those rules. She'd loved teaching skiing and snowboarding and avalanche safety. She'd loved guiding clients. She wasn't sure she even *liked* being in charge.

However, she was making more money than she'd ever made on a job before. If she stuck with this, she could eventually afford to buy one of the houses in Sultan's new low-income housing development. Owners contributed sweat, helping build their homes, and ended up with manageable mortgages as a result.

Yes, if she married Seamus she wouldn't have to worry about buying a house. And, yes, she would inherit her grandmother's house one day. But Rory wasn't used to looking at things that way—thinking in terms of what someone else could give her. She was used to figuring out what she could manage for herself.

Seamus said, "On Sunday, Fiona is willing to stay with the kids. I thought I'd like to come and see you in Sultan. But if you have tomorrow off..."

He'd already come to Sultan once, since their falling-out at the hospital. He'd also been to Montrose to pay an extra visit to her father, so that he could assure Rory that Kurt was regaining his strength and health. In Sultan, they'd skied together and eaten dinner, but he'd needed to return to Telluride that night.

"Can you stay in Telluride tomorrow night?" he asked.

"I think so. I'll double-check with Carrie, but I think that will work."

"Then we'll see you at the house at, say, five?"

"Great."

LAUREN APPEARED IN the kitchen early Saturday morning, the day of her fifteenth birthday. She was an early riser even on weekends, always eager to be outdoors snowboarding or, in the summer, trail-running.

Seamus was at the table, writing, working on the Koneko story and drinking coffee. "Happy birthday," he said.

She started, actually jumped. "You remembered."

"I always remember."

"I thought Fiona did the remembering for you. Then you'd leave a gift on the table the night before."

"Well, I wanted to make sure I caught you this morning. I want to take you shopping."

"For what?"

"For your present."

"Whatever I want?"

He smiled slowly. "I don't think I. can promise that. But we'll try to find you something you like."

"Thank you."

He picked up a package that had been sitting on the chairs out of sight. It was long and cylindrical.

"What's this?" Lauren asked.

"Your big present. But since the finished version couldn't be ready for today, we prepared this for you in advance."

"*We?*" Lauren asked suspiciously. She came to the table and examined the package. The paper had Ki-Rin and other story characters drawn all over it. She unwrapped it carefully, and a poster unrolled.

Koneko: The Movie.

Her face registered nothing but shock and pleasure, and then her eyes suddenly grew moist. Seeing this, Seamus felt himself tearing up, as well.

"Dad!" she said.

That word. That seldom-spoken, long-missed word.

"Thank you!"

He stood up from the table so that he could hug her. She hugged him back.

"It's all about Koneko?" she said.

He nodded. "And how she became a demoness. It should be a terrific story. People like her already, and now they're really going to love her."

"I'm so excited." She gazed at the poster. Black-haired Koneko with her geisha-white face, pointed ears, large eyes, long nails and trademark dark blue costume.

"Any ideas what you'd like to commemorate your birthday, besides a movie?" he asked. "I thought maybe a nice piece of jewelry. Something you can keep forever. Or we can just go look around."

"I wouldn't mind art," she said. "Or clothes. But clothes are more temporary."

"Why don't we go when the stores open," he said, "and we'll have lunch out?"

She nodded enthusiastically.

"And Rory's going to join us for dinner," he said, not adding, *which I hope is all right*. He was not going to ask Lauren's permission to include Rory in their family.

He couldn't read her face. She simply shrugged. "Can I get this framed?" she asked about the poster.

"I will gladly take care of that for you. This is obviously a prototype, and probably the real poster won't look like that."

"That makes this better."

THE MAIL ARRIVED before noon, carrying Lauren's birthday gift from Janine's parents. They often sent her clothing from posh department stores, usually preppy. Lauren always liked what they sent, so she turned to the package with interest. Beau, who was in the kitchen with Seamus at the time, watched as she began to open it. He usually received the same type of garment, which never went over as well with him as it did with Lauren. He preferred to buy his clothing at thrift stores or get it out of the Telluride free box.

As usual, it was a clothing box, and Lauren lifted the lid to find a card on top of the tissue paper. She read it, said, "Oh, wow," then folded back the tissue to reveal a blue-and-white letter jacket. "It's Mom's letter jacket from school! She was varsity, like, everything."

Seamus's stomach twisted painfully. Resentment curled inside him before he could stop it.

Janine's parents had inserted her into this day.

Of course, that wasn't fair.

His own relationship with them was edgy. They blamed him for Janine's death. In their eyes, it was his fault that she'd owned a gun. It was his fault that she'd felt the need for one. It was his fault for "letting" her buy one. It was his fault for not teaching her "how to use it correctly."

These things had been said, both obliquely and directly, and Seamus hadn't forgotten. Why would he? Neither parent had ever apologized for saying them, even after learning that Seamus had never seen any need for her to own a handgun, had objected to her buying one and knew almost nothing about guns himself.

A letter jacket. Lauren had already slipped it on. Her mother had gone to school in the Midwest. Coincidentally, the colors of her jacket were the same as Telluride's.

It makes her happy, Seamus thought, and he told himself that the fact should be enough to make him happy.

But instead it had the reverse effect. He did not want this reminder of Janine today, and he disliked himself for the feeling. He knew that the kids had told their grandparents he was planning to marry again—Lauren, in fact, had mentioned it to them before he'd thought to do so. Part of him believed that their reaction might have something to do with giving Janine's letter jacket to her oldest daughter this year.

Would he have felt differently about the gift if his engagement to Rory was still definitely on and if Lauren was happy about the idea of his marrying Rory? Perhaps. But that wasn't the case.

As predicted, Lauren wore the jacket on their shopping trip. Seamus did his best to put it out of his mind, asking her where she'd like to go first. "One of the galleries?" she suggested.

He nodded, and remembered shopping with Rory for the engagement ring he now kept for her. He would hide it when they entered the gallery where he'd bought the ring.

What drew Lauren's interest surprised him. She was most drawn to several metal sculptures of powerful-looking women. One carried a bow and arrow. It was almost a foot tall and cost a small fortune. "It's Artemis," she said. "It reminds me of Mom."

He harnessed his self-control, silently praying he wouldn't have to pay for a reminder of Janine—not this one anyhow. "Tell me how she's like Mom. Who was Artemis, again?"

"The Huntress. She was Apollo's twin. She was a virgin, and when men pursued her she turned them into stags and hunted them with her bow and arrow."

Seamus smiled in spite of himself and breathed his relief when she moved to the next statue. "But I like this one better. It's Freya. She's the Norse goddess of love. She's got her lynxes with her. They draw her chariot."

Seamus watched his daughter's eyes caress the statue.

"I know it's too much money," she said resignedly.

Seamus asked, "Is it what you want?"

"Yes." Her eyes shone.

The gallery owner wrapped it for them, but when they'd settled at their table at the restaurant Lauren had chosen for lunch, she carefully unwrapped it again and set it out to gaze at it. Then, she proceeded to tell her father of Freya's notoriously licentious behavior until he began to wonder if maybe she wouldn't have been better off with the virgin goddess, Artemis.

Recalling the analogy Lauren had drawn, Seamus asked, "You think your mom outran men?"

"Well, not exactly that. She just...didn't trust them completely. You know."

Janine had died when Lauren was only ten, and yet Lauren had perceived this.

"She must have trusted you, though," Lauren said. "I mean..." She frowned, thinking. "Well, not like you'd hurt her. But I don't think she trusted anyone but herself to protect herself."

"I think you're right about that." Which was why Janine had bought a handgun.

Maybe.

Because one part of him still believed that Janine simply had wanted people to know that she was the kind of person who had a handgun and knew how to use it.

Lauren smiled at the sculpture of Freya. "She always told me I had to protect myself, that I had to be smart." The corners of her mouth fell. "I'm not sure I'm so good at that."

Seamus was surprised by the maturity of this admission. "Then listen to your father," he said with a smile. The topic of Janine and the concept of a child protecting herself had the potential to ruin the rest of his day. He tried to think of all the things he'd wanted to tell Lauren today and now he wished that he'd written her a letter, written down all those things. If he spoke them, his words would be less perfect.

He could only try.

"Lauren, I want you to remember that you're a precious individual. You are yourself, and I'm proud of who you are and I like who you are. You never have to try to be like someone else." He was making a mess of it, he knew. He'd end up getting back to the topic he wanted to avoid, and at this point that could lead onto shaky ground.

"Like Mom," Lauren said. "You mean I don't need to be like Mom, and you don't want me to be. I know how she was. People always say, 'Your mom was one tough lady.' Or, 'Talk about a strong woman!' But you don't want me to be strong. Because you didn't like her."

"I definitely want you to be strong." *Leave it at that, Seamus. Leave it at that.* No need to say that Janine had been neither strong nor particularly ladylike.

No need to say that Lauren was right.

Or that, as of the day of her death, he hadn't liked Janine.

He'd only loved her.

"You can't hide it," Lauren said. "I know how you feel about her."

He knew that Lauren was intentionally provoking him. What he didn't know was why. "Can we drop this?" he asked.

She shrugged. "Sure. You want to forget her and replace her with Rory."

"I couldn't replace your mother, even if I wanted to. She is irreplaceable."

"Well, you've picked a woman who is

pretty much like her. Except Mom never did anything like dance. But she would have done fire-twirling and poi."

How well Lauren had known her mother. And how little she'd known her.

"I don't think Rory is like your mother." He repeated what he'd said before.

"Because you wouldn't want that. Someone who thinks for herself. You don't even want me thinking for myself."

"I do want you thinking for yourself, Lauren. I want you to think hard about the decisions you make. I want you to think before you lie about your age. I want you to think when you pick friends. And, yes, I want you to think for yourself—not just *act* for yourself."

To his surprise, Lauren gazed at him not angrily but with her brow furrowed, as if she'd actually heard him.

She said, "You think Mom was just acting for herself when she bought a gun."

"Pretty much," he admitted. "Lauren, this is not a good subject for me. I don't want to get angry, but now I *am* angry. I'm angry at the way your mother died—because it was a senseless event that should never have happened. It even makes me crazy that there's no better word than 'accident' to describe it. Do you understand what I'm saying?"

"No. It was an accident."

"It was stupid."

The waitress who'd brought their menus neared their table, and he said to her, "We haven't even looked at them." He turned back to Lauren. Now that he'd begun, he couldn't stop himself.

"It was stupid for her to buy a handgun, with four children in the house. It was stupid for her to carry it around with her. And ultimately, it was colossally stupid to pull that trigger *assuming* the gun wasn't loaded, and in a place where a bullet could ricochet with lethal consequences. Accidents are accidents. But what she did was something else."

It happened, then.

Lauren's eyes filled with tears, and he felt his own eyes sting. He had known he was losing control as it was happening, and still he'd been unable to stop himself from saying these things. He whispered, with some effort to make it right, "Lauren, she was too smart to behave that way. *Don't be like her.*" Oh, no, he shouldn't have said that, either—but he'd needed to say it, and he longed to say more. *Don't be insecure and pigheaded and boastful and reckless.*

Tears ran down Lauren's face, and she raised her napkin to her cheeks.

"Lauren," he said and reached across the table. He touched her forearm, but she shook her head, covering her face.

"I'm sorry," she whispered back, choked and incoherent. "I'm sorry I made you mad again."

We have to stop this, was all he could think. He tried to remember a single good thing to say about Janine, to make up for his torrent of criticism. "I loved it," he said, "when she made me laugh. And there were times when I even loved her brashness, because that made me laugh, too."

"Like when?"

"Like when we were in a lift line and some jerk coming off a run too fast almost ran her over, and she yelled at him to get a Seeing Eye dog. There were some completely shocked tourists beside us, who were horrified by the fact those words had come from the mouth of this beautiful blond woman."

Lauren laughed tearfully into her napkin.

He said, "I *did* like it that she would speak her mind. She didn't hesitate to tell people when she thought they were doing something wrong. She was less afraid of giving offense than of seeing tragic mistakes happen." Which was an irony to end all ironies.

Lauren was drying her eyes. She said, "Okay."

He didn't know what that meant. Did it mean, *Okay, you loved her?* Did it mean that his daughter was now okay?

After a tactful break of several minutes, the waitress returned to their table, and by then they were ready to order. "Great sculpture," she said, admiring Freya.

"She picked it out," Seamus said, "for her birthday."

"Good taste! Is this sixteenth?" she asked.

Lauren smiled and shook her head. "I'm fifteen."

RORY WAS BOTH tense and excited as she drove up to the yellow house. She'd spent that morning picking out some of her favorite belly-dance gear to give to Lauren. There were black flare pants with red tassels, an embroidered belt, dangling Bedouin earrings, a coin bra adorned with cowrie shells, a brilliant silk spinning skirt, a black Indian top and some cowrie shell hair ornaments. She had wrapped everything in purple tissue paper and packed it all inside the box her own telemark boots had come in, then wrapped the box in brown paper and tied it with twine interwoven with feathers and beads. Down at the coffeehouse, she'd found the perfect card.

She loved Lauren, and she wanted Lauren's friendship and allegiance; she wanted Lauren to want her for a stepmother. It felt imperative to win over the teenager. The other three children seemed to accept her, and seemed glad to have her in their lives. *Please let Lauren be happy to have me around.*

As she climbed out of her car, Seuss ran from the back door. One of his ears was half folded over, making him look especially sweet. "Hi, Seuss," she cried and knelt down to hug the puppy. *If things don't work out with Seamus,* she thought, *I'll get another dog.*

Once she had a more permanent home.

But she wanted things to work out with Seamus and she liked this dog a lot.

Beau followed Seuss outside. "Hi, Rory."

"Hi." She took the package out of the car.

"What'd you get her?" Beau asked.

"It's a secret until she opens it."

"No fair," he said.

"That's life. How's Seuss doing? His manners seem pretty good. I could tell he was trying hard not to jump on me."

"He still does sometimes. He likes to put his paws on my shoulders. The obedience teacher here says I can teach him to do that on command. There are *fifteen* dogs in the class."

"That's a ton."

"Well, there are lots of dogs in Telluride."

Rory followed Beau and the puppy through the mudroom. *This is where Janine died,* she thought again, marveling that the Lees lived here and used this room as though nothing tragic had happened there.

"Hi," Seamus greeted her as she entered the kitchen. He hugged her and kissed her and touched her hair, which was loose. "You're wearing a dress."

"I've been known to do that." It was a flowing A-line dress in red. Over it, she wore a wool coat that had been her grandmother's, and on her feet were ankle-high boots. There was still snow on the ground, both in Sultan and in Telluride.

Lauren entered the kitchen. She wore a letter jacket that Rory assumed was her own until Lauren came over and said, "Look what my grandparents sent me. It was my mom's."

Seamus turned away, grabbing a coffee mug from a hook as he said, "Like an espresso, Rory? I think I'll have one."

"Yes, please. That sounds great. Happy birthday, Lauren. Are those Telluride colors, too?"

"Yes. Perfect, huh?"

Rory nodded. Lauren had done it deliberately, shown her *this* gift. It was unfair and unkind, but that didn't matter. Lauren was still growing up. Rory handed her the wrapped box.

"Oh, thanks," Lauren said. "Should I open it now?"

"You can."

Belle came into the kitchen then, yelling, "Rory!"

"Hey, you're wearing a red dress, too,"

Rory said, picking her up and hugging her. "We match."

"Cute," Lauren said without inflection, moving toward the kitchen table.

As Caleb and Fiona joined them, Lauren began to open her card. Rory watched her look at it and read it, her head down, her face showing nothing. "Thanks," she said, laying it aside.

She unwrapped the box next, and opened the lid.

The coin bra was on top. She took it out slowly, her expression unchanging. "I think it will fit," Rory said, joining Lauren at the table. "We're about the same size."

Lauren held it up against herself experimentally. "Yeah," she agreed.

Rory watched her unwrap all the other gifts, too, and then put them back in the box.

"Thank you," Lauren said. "That's really nice."

Rory thought, for a moment, about the fact that the coin bra had cost her $200 when she bought it four years ago. Lauren knew this because the two of them had discussed costuming and the pleasures of acquiring costume pieces for tribal belly dance. Rory had bought the earrings at an antique store in Denver. She'd given Lauren some of her *treasures.* And received very little acknowledgment of that.

Oh, well.

"There are belly dance classes here," Lauren said. "They're cabaret style."

"Some of those pieces will cross over," Rory told her.

"No, it's completely different. But thanks."

I don't deserve this, Rory thought. She heard the espresso machine hiss.

"A latte okay?" Seamus asked.

Rory walked over to him. "Thank you."

He put his arm around her shoulders. "That was a generous gift. Were those out of your personal trove?"

"Yes. I like the idea of Lauren having them."

Lauren had closed the lid on the box. "I'm going upstairs to change," she said, and walked out of the kitchen without the box.

Seamus's hand on Rory's shoulder gently soothed her. He rested his head against hers, and she felt his lips brush her hair.

He understood.

Rory hugged his waist. "How was your shopping trip?"

He gave her a look. "Tell you about it later. She found something she really likes." Under the sound of the espresso machine, so that Fiona and the children couldn't hear, he said, "If she weren't punishing us, I think she'd have shown it to you instead of the letter jacket."

Rory saw the engagement ring on his finger. She said, "Mind if I wear that?"

"You've missed me." He turned toward her with a broad grin. He said, "Just want to wear it for a while?"

"While I'm here."

"That works." He took it off his finger and slid it onto hers.

She swallowed.

Seuss had brought his ball into the kitchen. It bounced through the door, and Belle and Caleb and Beau all followed the dog as he chased it. Fiona said, "Well, I'll say good night. I'm going to my room."

"Good night, Fiona." Rory hugged her impulsively. "You're not coming out to dinner?"

"Lauren said it was all right if I wanted to stay here. And I do."

As she left the kitchen, Seamus said, "She told me that she thinks this should be a family night. I told her that she is family, but she shook her head and said she thought it should just be the six of us."

"I like her a lot," Rory said.

"Who wouldn't?"

"Yes. Quite." Rory hesitated, gazing at the ring on her hand, and said hesitantly, "Whenever I put this on, I'm afraid, Seamus."

He turned to her. "Of what?" He handed her the latte.

"Thanks, it's perfect. If Ki-Rin ever gets too old, you have a great future as a barista."

"Ha ha. Afraid of what?" he repeated.

"Not sure. I wonder if it has anything to do with my job history."

He folded his arms across his chest. "Now, this is a theory to hear."

"Don't make fun of me. It's just…I can't seem to keep a job. And I'm not sure I like my new one, by the way. But I'm wondering if I've set myself up to lose jobs in the past. And if I'm afraid to stick with anything. And marriage is certainly sticking with something."

"You stick with belly dance and fire dance."

"True." She shook her head. "I don't understand it. I love you and I love your children, and I can actually *picture* us living happily together for the rest of our lives. But I'm anxious, and I don't know why. I just know I should pay attention to the feeling."

Seamus's stomach knotted. It wasn't that he wanted her to ignore her intuition. He simply wanted there to be no reason for her wariness. And there must be a reason. Intuition was the type of thing that could end their relationship. Because it probably represented something that was true.

Maybe there was a different future in store for Rory Gorenzi.

She said, "That probably doesn't exactly make your night."

"No. It doesn't," he agreed.

She embraced him again. "Maybe we should just keep seeing each other—without getting married."

He shrugged. "I'd be willing to try. Who knows? Maybe Lauren would be easier with that."

"If my dad takes over the school again," Rory said, "I'm prepared to come here."

He held her and kissed the crown of her head. "Thank you," he said. "Thank you."

CHAPTER FOURTEEN

WHEN KURT RETURNED to Sultan three weeks after his surgery, Rory told him of her decision. "I've told Seamus I'll move to Telluride. Just…after you're able to take the reins again."

"When's the wedding?"

"I'm not sure."

"Why aren't you sure?" Her father's expression was keen. He sat on the front porch of the small cabin that had always been his, in a green rocking chair. Sultan's dirt roads were a mess of slush and mud. Rory had walked to her dad's on foot, and her boots were caked with the mud.

Evading, she said, "Oh—I just want to know what's happening here. There's no rush."

"You've got cold feet, haven't you?" her father said.

Considering his earlier prognostications

on the subject, this was quite a turnaround. "What makes you think that?"

"We talked at the hospital, he and I."

Rory shrugged. "There are just so many things up in the air. I have to confess, I don't think I'm cut out to manage the school. I like being in the field and I like teaching. I *can* be an administrator, but I don't care for it."

"What's bothering you about committing yourself to him?"

"Intuition, maybe. It's not about him, anyhow. There's just something that's not right."

"That's a good thing to pay attention to." Her father's expression showed regret, whether because of her doubts or his own history, she couldn't guess.

"What was your intuition," Rory said, "before you married my mother?"

"To be perfectly honest, I didn't have a moment's doubt. I don't regret having married her, Rory, any more than I regret that we had you."

But he was a proud man, she knew, and her mother had been unfaithful.

Strangely, none of her doubts extended to the idea of living with Seamus and his family, even for the rest of her life. It was the thought of marriage. To anyone.

And she didn't understand why she should feel that way.

She told her father this.

He laughed. "I understand why you might feel that way. Your own parents' marriage didn't have a happy ending. And you were raised by a single woman—a widow, yes, but also a woman disinclined to marry again."

"That's not enough to explain it. Maybe there's some purpose in store for me that precludes marriage. Or that marriage would preclude."

"I do know this," Kurt said. "You can be a couple for ten years, but it's not the same relationship you have after you say, 'I do.'"

And that, Rory realized, was what frightened her. That she had no idea what would follow, if she said those words to Seamus.

But suddenly things fell into place for Rory. She'd never run from what frightened her, just because it was unknown, and she wasn't about to run this time. She would marry Seamus Lee as soon as he was ready. It was what she wanted, too.

She fingered the ring that was still on her finger.

"Thank you," she said. "This probably sounds crazy, but what you've said actually helped."

THEY SET THE DATE for June twenty-first. The wedding would be in Sultan, outdoors if the weather permitted, in a meadow a few hundred feet above the town.

Seamus told his children all together, as he'd told them of the engagement, on a Saturday in May. Rory was coming to Telluride to go for a hike with him and the three younger children. Lauren said she didn't want to go.

After telling them of the wedding date, the boys and Belle wandered off to pursue their own interests while Lauren lingered behind with her father.

The two had maintained a shaky peace ever since Lauren's birthday. She wore Janine's letter jacket every day, and Seamus wasn't even sure that she liked it. He knew she hadn't forgotten the things he'd said at lunch that day. After such arguments, she always seemed remorseful and appeared to take the blame for making him angry.

At those times, he felt hope that she *understood* that her mother hadn't necessarily always been someone to emulate. But then her attitude would change again and they'd be back to square one. Rory's birthday present remained in its box, stacked on top of a pile of books in one corner of her room, as if forgotten.

It puzzled Seamus that Lauren could be so disinterested in this gift, when she had previously been so taken with belly dance and fire-twirling. She *had* liked Rory—until Rory had agreed to marry her father.

Now, Seamus pointed this out.

"There wasn't anything else to do in Sultan," Lauren said morosely. "Look, lots of women like you, Dad, and I'm sure they know that liking us is also some kind of requirement for landing you. You know, making things permanent. And sure, I believe she actually likes us, but it was pretty clear that the two of you were mostly into each other. Anyhow, I know you're not going to do what I say, but, no, I don't want you to marry her. We don't *need* her."

"I'm not sure your brothers and sister would agree with that."

"Oh, they *like* her. But they don't really care one way or another what you decide."

"Why don't you want me to marry her?"

Lauren shook her head, looking exasperated. "It's just like you want someone on your *side*."

"My side in what?"

"Against Mom. You wanted to divorce her. I know that, and you can't hide it or deny it."

She was right, he silently acknowledged. He had, by the end, wanted to divorce his wife.

"So it's really like my parents are divorced," Lauren said, "except that my mother is actually dead, and my father doesn't miss her. And he gets to write history the way he wants, because she can't defend herself."

Her interpretation staggered him—particularly the accusation of rewriting history.

She said, "I suppose we'll be moving to Sultan, now."

"I haven't decided about that."

"It would be okay," she said. "I mean, it's not like there are any guys I like here who are my age, either. At least there…" Her voice drifted off. Clearly, she feared she'd said too much. She shook her head.

Seamus waited.

"I just wish we could move there *without* Rory being part of it. I wish you thought we were enough for you."

"It's not a question of your not being enough. I fell in love with Rory, and not least because she loves all of you. I realized I wanted to spend the rest of my life with her."

"What if she starts doing things you don't like, the way Mom did?"

Seamus considered this. When *had* he begun thinking about divorcing Janine? Not until she'd bought the gun? Was it just that one issue? No. But it was the gun that had made him think there might be no way other than divorce to get past their differences. He'd known, however, that even if they were divorced, she would still own a gun and sometimes the children would be in a home where a gun was kept.

"I'm sure there will be times when she does things I don't like. That's part of marriage."

"She's not as smart as Mom. Mom was an attorney. Rory's just had a bunch of blue-collar jobs."

Seamus decided to let that pass for the moment. "Lauren," he said, "I love Rory, I plan to marry her, and I expect you to respect her and treat her courteously. You will be part of our family and go where we go."

He watched her, waiting.

She said, "Fine. Whatever."

BEAU AND SEUSS RACED up to Rory when she arrived. As she got out of her car, Beau said, "Watch this." He crouched in front of Seuss, who was stamping his forefeet impatiently. "Seuss, hug."

The German shepherd put his paws on Beau's shoulders and licked his face.

Rory grinned broadly. "You are so good with him, Beau. He's a good puppy, and he's going to be a great dog, the way you work with him."

Beau's eyes rested on Seuss with pride.

They went into the house together through the front door and followed the sound of voices to the kitchen.

Lauren said, "You said you don't want me to be like Mom. You don't even respect her that much."

Rory hung back.

Beau's eyes shifted right and left, and he dropped his head.

"But I *am* like her, and I *want* to be. You just demean her."

Seamus glanced up. "Rory. Beau."

Lauren spun around, unfazed to learn she'd been overheard.

Beau stepped toward his sister. "Why don't you give it up, Lauren? You didn't even see what she did to herself."

Rory saw Seamus freeze and she knew what must be running through his mind. She stared at Beau as his father said to him, "Neither did you."

Beau met Seamus's eyes and he looked as if he might flee. From what?

"You were outside," Seamus said.

Beau seemed to consider whether or not to speak. "I went in the French doors."

Seamus turned white. "The police never told me."

"They were mad."

"I *wanted* to see her," Lauren said.

Rory couldn't believe what she was hearing. Beau had seen what Seamus had seen.

"There was so much blood. The bullet went right through her neck," Beau told his sister. "You're being stupid, just like her. You don't even know what guns do. Why do you think we had to stay in a hotel for three days? It wasn't just because she died in the house. They had to clean up the blood! They even painted. Don't you remember the paint?"

Rory moved close to Beau and put her hands on his shoulders. He was shaking violently. "Two of my friends weren't even allowed to come over here because their parents knew Mom had a gun. I told her that, and she just looked at me and said, 'Oh, well.' That's what she said, Lauren!"

Lauren stood stock still. "You're all ganging up on her. Nobody loves her but me."

Lauren's words terrified Seamus. There was a desperate finality in them, a conclusion that it was Lauren and the memory of Janine against the entire world. A conclusion that Lauren was utterly alone and had no allies.

He said, "Beau, please take back what you said about your mother and your sister."

Beau burst into tears, broke away from Rory and fled. The front door slammed behind him.

"He only said what you think!" Lauren accused.

Seamus hated that part of this accusation was true.

Rory said, "I'm going to check on Beau."

"He's only started to act this way about her since you appeared," Lauren said. She was speaking to Rory, and "he" was Seamus.

Rory walked out of the kitchen and then out of the house, following Seamus's older son and his dog.

SEAMUS SAGGED AGAINST the counter, then went to the table and sat down. "You win, Lauren," he said.

"What do you mean?" She was sneering.

"We'll remember your mother the way you want," he said, hardly understanding what he was saying, knowing only that he could not let his daughter believe herself isolated from the rest of her family.

"Beau was probably lying," she said somberly.

Seamus reached out for her hand and pulled her into the chair next to his. He waited for her to look at him.

"He wasn't lying," he said, and he reached out and hugged his daughter. "I didn't want any of you to see what I saw, and I don't think it's good at all for Beau that he saw it. I think he's probably going to have to talk to someone about it."

"Like a psychiatrist?"

Pulling back, Seamus shook his head. "A grief counselor. Or someone who's the right person for a boy his age. Lauren, would you like someone like that to talk to? Someone who listens to you and sympathizes with you and isn't offended when you tell her your feelings?"

"If you're talking about Rory…"

He shook his head again. "I'm talking about a counselor, Lauren. And Lauren, I meant what I said. I'll help you remember your mother in the way that's true for you. It's wrong of me to do anything else."

"But you think it's a lie."

He considered. "No. I think it's who she is to you, and no one has the right to take that away from you. I know I don't."

Lauren leaned forward, and he realized that his daughter wanted his embrace again.

So he held her and said, "You're a wonderful person, Lauren. And if you're like your mom, that's a credit to both of you." He had thought he would choke on the words, but as he spoke them he realized it wasn't so hard. She was still a child, and he didn't have to tell her lies about Janine—and he didn't have to tell her the truth. She was going to idealize Janine, for now, and maybe forever.

He said, "Lauren, I have to check on Beau now. You understand?"

She nodded.

He left her and followed Rory to find his son.

THEY WERE UNDERNEATH the tree house Seamus had built when Beau was quite young. They sat on a fallen tree trunk that had been converted to a bench. Rory, with her hair in a loose braid, wearing Carhartt shorts, T-shirt and hiking boots, looked like a teenager herself.

They saw him coming. Beau was wiping his eyes.

Seamus neared them and crouched in front of his son. "I wish you'd told me."

"I didn't want to get in trouble. The marshals had already yelled at me."

"I understand."

"Why did I look?"

"It's pretty natural."

"But she was my mom! Why did I want to see that?"

"You didn't," Seamus answered. "You didn't know what you would see."

Rory said, "Beau thinks it would be okay to talk to a counselor about this."

And Lauren said Rory isn't smart, Seamus thought. Well, she had enough common sense for him; enough common sense to see that his children couldn't handle this alone.

Just as she'd helped him see that he couldn't, either.

That he couldn't live life alone.

THAT EVENING, RORY knocked on Lauren's door.

Again, she heard the teenager standing up, coming to the door. Lauren wasn't someone who just called out an invitation to enter.

She looked at Rory.

Rory asked, "May I come in?"

Lauren shrugged and turned away.

Rory entered the room and sat down in a white leather chair. "This is comfortable," she exclaimed in surprise.

"I like to sit in it when I study," Lauren said.

"I want to know if you've been practicing with your staff."

Lauren shook her head. "Not much."

Rory said, "Remember how you said you'd like to be part of a troupe?"

Lauren looked as if she regretted the words and the thought. "You said I'm not ready."

"Well, kind of. Not for lighting fire, yet. You really have to be good with your props before you add fire to what you're doing. But while I was running the school for my dad I couldn't teach dance anymore. I just didn't have the time or energy. So Samantha started doing it. And she's got two pretty enthusiastic beginning students. But we think five is a good number for a troupe. And you're naturally graceful and a good athlete. You can do isolations. Your body works well for this. I just thought if you wanted to practice regularly..."

"You're bribing me."

Rory's eyes shifted sideways, then back. "Well, let's put it this way. If you hadn't gotten mad at me for agreeing to marry your dad, I would have asked you, anyway. If you were going to be in Sultan."

"What if we stay here?" Lauren asked.

"Then, I think we need to get some tribal fusion belly dance going in Telluride. Did you mean, by the way, that you like cabaret style?"

Lauren made a face. And didn't answer.

Rory took that for *No*. As in, *I said that just to hurt you*.

Lauren said, "Doesn't it seem weird to you that my dad wanted to stay in this house?"

"He might have thought it was best for the four of you. So that you wouldn't lose both your mom and your home."

Lauren said, "I guess. I didn't want to move. I just wanted my mom back."

"I wish you had her back," Rory said. "I didn't know my mom, except when I was a baby. I don't remember her at all."

"Your mom died?" Lauren asked.

Rory nodded. "In a skiing accident. But it was when I was too little to remember anything."

Lauren thought for a minute, and Rory could imagine what she was thinking. Was it better to have loved and lost...? Rory *did* love her mother, but that was an incomplete feeling. She didn't have a single memory of her. Only an emptiness.

Rory said, "Will you please dance and do staff-twirling with me again? If I move here, I won't have anyone to dance with, and dancing with other people is what's the most fun for me."

"Okay." Lauren nodded.

"Have you tried on the stuff I gave you?"

Lauren shook her head.

"Maybe another day?" Rory asked.

"Or, like, tonight. If you stay tonight. You're probably staying, right?"

Rory nodded. "Thank you, Lauren."

CHAPTER FIFTEEN

On June fourth, Caleb's birthday, Rory joined Lauren outside the house. The two of them were going to take Caleb downtown while Seamus put the finishing touches on his son's present, a set of skateboard obstacles that could be used on the garage floor or outside in winter with Caleb's snowskate.

Lauren's attitude toward Rory had mellowed slightly. During the three dance practice sessions they'd fit into Rory's work schedule, the teenager hadn't exuded the warmth and enthusiasm she'd originally showed. Still, Rory thought that even if Lauren wasn't *encouraging* marriage between her father and Rory, she was at least grudgingly accepting it.

Now, Lauren asked with her typical lack of enthusiasm, "Did you get Caleb anything?"

Rory nodded. In a low voice, she said, "Just

this snowboard/skater sweatshirt he admired in Sultan. I hope he still likes it."

"Is it pink?" Lauren asked. Her brother loved shocking pink and wore it with enthusiasm. He was a strong athlete and popular and he knew it. The bright pink was a reflection of that confidence.

"Black and pink. Yes." Rory smiled.

"He'll like it," Lauren said.

"What about you?"

"I got him a CD. I already gave it to him. I hate his taste in music, but it's his birthday. You know."

"You're a good sister," Rory said. "You really take care of all of them."

"Well…not Beau," Lauren pointed out.

"That's true." Both Lauren and Beau had entered counseling, and Seamus had gone to one session on his own. Rory wanted to ask Lauren about her counselor, if she liked the woman, that kind of thing, but it felt too much like prying into something private.

"You spend more time with us than with Dad," Lauren observed.

It wasn't so, of course, because every time she came to Telluride, Rory spent the evening with Seamus, touching, laughing and making plans for the future. She said now, "I see plenty of him. I'll be glad when my dad can be back at work all the time, though." She'd cut her hours to four days a week, which left her more time to be with the Lees, but Kurt Gorenzi still had not regained his strength completely. Where he had previously seemed young and vital, suddenly he had aged.

Rory saw difficult choices ahead. He was going to have to find a partner in the Sultan Mountain School, or hire someone to take over as director for him. If family life allowed, Rory could be a partner in running the school. She did not want the directorship, however; not on her own.

Seamus had been looking at property in Sultan. He'd concluded that he could open a second work location in Sultan. The offices could send files via e-mail and by courier; it could work.

Rory found that, as sensitive as Seamus initially had been about her accepting the job her father had offered, now he was willing to compromise. He saw that her father's health wasn't good, and he was more willing to make it possible for her to help at the Sultan Mountain School. Lauren, too, seemed less adamant about remaining in Telluride. She and Beau and Caleb and Belle had accompanied Seamus on a tour of the K-12 Sultan school the previous week. Lauren had said it "seemed all right."

Now, Rory asked her, "Lauren, would you like to be in the wedding?"

Lauren shook her head. "Not really."

Samantha and one of Seamus's employees would be maid of honor and best man, respectively. Rory had selected a fairly simple ivory dress. It was long-sleeved and should be warm enough for an outdoor ceremony, even at high altitude. She planned to wear a wreath on her head. Neither she nor Seamus wanted an elaborate ceremony. They'd invited family, his employees and a few close friends. A local minister in Sultan would perform the ceremony.

Caleb came out of the house with Seuss on a leash.

Lauren said, "We shouldn't take him. He won't be able to go in stores and stuff."

"We can tie him up outside," Caleb said.

Rory hesitated. While it was good for a dog to be able to wait courteously outside a building, it was also a good way for a dog to be stolen. She pointed this out to Caleb.

Caleb said, "I guess you're right. C'mon boy." He took the dog back inside, then ran out again to join his sister and Rory.

They climbed into Rory's car and drove downtown. They'd promised to take Caleb to the Telluride Skate Park and also to a bookstore, so he could use the gift certificate Fiona had given him.

They parked the car and walked to the skate park, where Rory sat watching Caleb while Lauren walked across the grass to a friend's house, which adjoined the park. The friend was named Cassidy and Rory had met her only once, briefly. Lauren promised to be back in half an hour.

Caleb had the park almost completely to himself. He came over to Rory's bench to ask her to watch one trick or another and to time him crossing the big bowl and coming back. She was doing this when she heard what sounded like the report of a gun.

It had come from the houses near the park and terror immediately seized her. Where was Lauren?

"Caleb," she called and waved him over as

she stood up. She gazed toward the houses just as Lauren came out of her friend's house. Lauren, too, was glancing around, looking for the source of the gunfire.

She crossed the lawn to Rory and Caleb, looking back over her shoulder.

"Probably someone cleaning a weapon," Rory said uneasily.

Lauren hugged herself, and for a moment they all stood gazing toward the houses, waiting uneasily. Caleb stood on his skateboard and practiced ollies in place, until Rory said, "Let's get on to the bookstore, Caleb."

They walked back into town, and then to the bookstore. Lauren was uncharacteristically pale and quiet.

Rory said, "Was Cassidy there?"

"Oh. Yes." Lauren nodded abruptly, seeming preoccupied.

"You okay?" Rory asked.

Lauren nodded again. "Fine."

A sound on the street. Maybe it could have been a car backfiring. But Rory felt sure that Lauren's thoughts had turned to handguns; to the possibility of an accident somewhere, an accident like her mother's or with equally tragic consequences.

"Want to have a chai or something, while Caleb looks at books?"

"Yes," Lauren said. "Maybe a frozen chai. It's kind of warm out." And yet she shivered, rubbing her arms.

In the bookstore, while Caleb wandered the kids' section, then began looking at books of photos, Rory and Lauren sat at a table in the back, near the espresso counter. Rory ordered a latte and Lauren a frozen chai, and they sat together sipping them.

A siren cut through the sounds of the store, the sounds outside.

"Oh, no," Lauren said.

Rory instinctively grasped her forearm. "It's probably not related."

"You're thinking about it, too," Lauren observed.

"Well...yes."

The barista, overhearing them, said, "That's a fire truck."

"You're sure?" Lauren looked toward her, anxious.

The woman nodded. "Yeah. I'm on the ambulance crew. You learn the different sirens. That's the fire guys."

"Not related," Rory repeated.

Lauren nodded, then drew on her straw. She said, "I can do that whole fire staff routine three times in a row without a mistake."

"Really?" Rory knew, as Lauren did, that this was the forerunner to being able to use a lighted staff. She said, "I'm willing to ask your dad if you can work with a lit staff, but you have to make me a few promises first."

Lauren waited.

"Absolutely no alcohol or drugs and fire arts together," Rory said. "I mean it, Lauren. We're going to look at some pictures of the burns people get, so you appreciate this."

"It would be really dumb," Lauren said. "I don't do that stuff, anyhow. I don't like feeling out of control."

"Me, either," Rory agreed fervently. "And don't get in cars with drunk people or people on drugs."

"I know," Lauren said.

"The other thing is, no fire arts unless I'm there. This isn't something to, like, show your friends you can do. You need to be with other people who are part of your team and who have a lot of experience. Usually, I completely discourage people under eighteen from using fire. I would only do this because

I know you very well and *trust* you to only do it when I'm there."

Lauren nodded.

"There are all sorts of protocols for using fire," Rory continued, "and we have to follow them precisely. Things like tying up your hair and getting it completely wet. Having a spotter with a fire blanket. Sometimes people think it's just as safe to use a wet towel, but you can get really bad steam burns that way. And how you deal with fuels on the wicks takes experience. There's no other way, or you can have lit drops of kerosene flying everywhere, burning people or starting fires."

Lauren looked appropriately apprehensive.

"So, that rule of doing it only when I'm there with you, supervising, is absolute."

"What about, say, Samantha?"

"Actually, no. Samantha *does* know what she's doing, but she's not a guardian for you. When I marry your dad, I will be."

"Okay," Lauren agreed.

Her eyes suddenly drifted away, looking in the direction of the skate park as if she could see through walls and buildings to the source of the gunshot they'd heard.

She said, "I'm not sure I want to do it with fire."

"Good," Rory answered. "I'm really happy to hear you say that."

"Why?"

"It's something to be afraid of. Fear isn't bad. It keeps you alive and healthy."

Lauren nodded, lowering her eyes.

Caleb came over to their table with a book called *Off the Map,* which showed objects on the earth photographed from space. "Found it," he said. "Can I have a chai?"

THAT EVENING, THEY sat around the large-screen television upstairs to watch *Harry Potter and the Deathly Hallows—Part 2.* Belle was already asleep, having accepted the fact that the movie had "scary parts." Rory leaned against Seamus on the couch, and Lauren, Beau and Caleb flopped on big pillows on the floor.

Just after the opening credits, Lauren's cell phone rang. She looked at the number, made a face and said, "Don't pause it." She stood up and walked into the other room.

Rory followed her with her eyes, and Seamus looked at Rory's face. "Everything all right?"

It was one of those tingling feelings.

Lauren didn't return for several minutes, and Seamus stood up to see if she was still on the phone. The light was on in her bathroom, and he heard her retching through the door.

He knocked. "Lauren?"

"Yes," came through the door.

"Can I come in?"

"Yes," again.

She was kneeling in front of the toilet, her eyes filled with tears.

"Are you sick?" Seamus asked.

She shook her head and seemed unable to speak. Her eyes were wide and stricken.

He crouched beside her. "What is it? Tell me."

She only shook her head.

Rory came into the bathroom behind him. "What is it, Lauren?"

"The shot," Lauren said to her.

Rory, too, crouched beside her. "What was it?"

"A guy shot an oil lamp in his wife's house. Or ex-wife or something."

Seamus frowned. He'd heard about this incident earlier in the day. The fire truck they'd heard had been responding to the fire that resulted. The estranged husband had been drunk and was violating a restraining order, but at least no one had been wounded. "No one was hurt, were they?" he said.

She shook her head, eyes wet.

Rory, on her knees beside her, hugged her. "That shot scared me, too, when I heard it," she said.

Seamus said, "Do you want to call Simone, Lauren?" Lauren's counselor.

Lauren shrugged. "Maybe." She held onto Rory.

Seamus rubbed his daughter's head. "Feel like watching the movie?"

Lauren nodded. She said, "I'm sorry, Dad."

"Don't be. None of this is your fault."

"What I said."

"When?" But he didn't need to hear the answer. He knew what she was sorry for. She was sorry for arguing with him about Janine's owning a handgun. She was sorry for loving her mother's memory.

"Stuff." She shook her head.

"Lauren," he told her, "your mom was

scared of people like that guy. And it's pretty normal to be scared."

She nodded and stood up slowly.

Rory, standing too, ran water in the sink. She suspected that Lauren's nausea had come from fear at the thought of the firearm the man had wielded—from realization of what a gun could do.

Lauren splashed water on her face and grabbed her toothbrush and the tube of toothpaste. "I'll be okay," she said.

"You *are* okay," Seamus told her. "You're very okay, Lauren Lee."

CHAPTER SIXTEEN

THEY WERE IN Sultan for the week, using the Empire Street house, with Kurt Gorenzi's blessing, during wedding preparations.

On the morning of the wedding, however, Lauren and Rory and Samantha were at Sondra Nichols's home helping Rory dress, while Belle played with her stuffed animals in the next room, when Rory's cell phone rang. Rory was at her dressing table and unable to move because both her grandmother and Lauren were holding up pieces of her hair.

"Should I answer?" asked Samantha.

"Yes, please."

"Hello? No, it's Samantha. Hi, Beau. No, she can't talk."

"I can," Rory said.

"*I'll* talk to him," Lauren said, as though prepared to sort out the brother who'd dared to call at such an inconvenient time.

Samantha took the part of Rory's hair

which Lauren had been holding and they traded the phone.

"What?" said Lauren. Then, "You're kidding. What did Dad say? Really? Okay. No, *I'll* tell her. She's getting her hair done. Bye."

She hung up. "Your old house is for sale again."

"Oh, yeah, I know," Samantha said. "The guy's business is tanking, and he needs cash right away."

"It's a cool house," Lauren said.

"For, like, a family of six," Samantha put in. "Maybe with a housekeeper thrown in." She laughed.

"What did your dad say?" Rory asked.

"That he won't live in a pink house."

Samantha and Rory made faces at each other. They'd always liked the exterior of Desert's house. Desert wasn't able to come back to Sultan for the wedding. She said her parents couldn't do without her, even for a few days.

Sondra said, "I should say not. That place looks garish. I was surprised the new owner didn't paint it first thing."

"That's part of its charm," Samantha told her.

They continued weaving the wreath into Rory's hair.

"Does he like the house except for its being pink?" Rory asked Lauren.

"Beau's not sure. The pink was the big deal. And Caleb likes it pink."

"I like pink, too." Belle came in carrying Mouse and Squish. Her dress was a child's version of Lauren's, in light blue. "So does Squish. Squish's tentacle got squished by Elsie Cow, and he needs it kissed."

"Didn't you kiss it?" Samantha asked.

"By Lauren."

"Oh." Her sister crouched down. "Which one was it?"

"I don't know," Belle said.

"Better get all of them," Samantha advised.

Belle nodded in agreement as the doorbell sounded.

Sondra made a perplexed face, then hurried to answer it. They heard her speaking to someone, and then she called, "Lauren, will you come here?"

Lauren left the bedroom, and Rory wondered who was there.

A moment later, the girl returned to the bedroom with Sondra behind her. Lauren carried a large white envelope, the size of a tabloid newspaper. Her eyes were bright, excited.

Rory looked up at her.

"I've been entrusted by Dad to give you your wedding present," Lauren told her. She placed the envelope on the table in front of Rory. "I'm supposed to explain it to you."

As Samantha finished her hair, Rory opened one end of the envelope and slid out the contents. It was a glossy image, a print, of an anime character with curly brown-and-gold hair and huge brown eyes. She was surrounded by fire and carried lit coals in each hand. Behind her loomed a massive yellow-and-white snake with red eyes. Lola with a cobra's hood and fangs, breathing fire.

"Her name is Mieko. She's a fire goddess. The snake is Tama. She protects Mieko. And Dad wanted you to be sure to know that he asked me and I said it's okay. In fact, we kind of came up with it together—Koneko was dedicated to the fire goddess as an infant. She chose to turn from that calling and become a demon. But Koneko is still tied to Mieko, and she can never break that bond, and Mieko watches over her and sometimes calls her back from evil."

Rory's reflection swam in the mirror. Swallowing, she set the print against the glass as Samantha pinned the wreath to her head.

Rory said to Lauren, "Thank you," and reached a hand toward the girl.

Lauren reached around from behind and hugged her. "You look pretty," she said.

RORY RODE TO Blythe Meadow in her father's Toyota Land Cruiser, with Belle and Lauren, while Sondra rode in Samantha's car.

My father is going to give me away on my wedding day. A year ago, none of it would have seemed possible. But now she was his partner at the Sultan Mountain School. She and Seamus had decided that the family would live in Sultan—all they needed was a suitable house.

Rory hoped that Desert's old house would meet the criteria, but there were other possibilities, as well, including building a new house—an idea her father embraced, of course, as a boost to Sultan's economy.

They reached the meadow, and Rory peered across the sunlit grass until she spotted Seamus in a tuxedo, speaking with the minister.

Beau ran toward the Land Cruiser and opened the door. "I'm helping you out," he told Rory.

"Thank you," she said and scanned the guests, waving to Sultan friends and turning toward Samantha's vehicle. "Will you go help my grandmother, too, Beau?"

"Yes." He shut her door behind her and ran toward Samantha's passenger door. Caleb beat him.

Kurt came around the front of his car and offered his arm to Rory.

"Thanks, Dad," she said.

The guests were nearly all seated in folding chairs set up in the meadow for the ceremony. She saw Jay Norris from the Sultan Mountain School ushering a woman in a head scarf and a man in a dark suit and yarmulke into seats on the bride's side.

"No way," Rory said.

"Yes, way," Samantha told her. "But you'll have to wait until after the ceremony to say hi. Just don't pass out when she introduces him."

"As?"

"The Rabbi David Stern, her *fiancé*."

Rory laughed out loud. "Is she still Desert?"

"Noami," Samantha said with a smile. "Though I get the feeling this guy might have some pretty sweet names for her when they're alone."

The recorded wedding march began to play on the car stereo that was serving as sound system. Seamus's best man offered his arm to Samantha, and they began the walk ahead of Rory and Kurt.

Kurt said to his daughter, "Well, I'm glad all my scheming paid off."

"What scheming?"

"My dear, what kind of generous soul do you think was going to give Seamus Lee and his kids the gift of a three-month course with the Sultan Mountain School?"

Rory gazed at her father, aghast. "Someone with ulterior motives, obviously."

"Well, *you* weren't part of the plan. Not exactly."

"What does that mean?" They needed to start walking, but she wanted to hear the answer to this.

"Let's go," said her father. As they took

the first steps that would lead her to the rest of her life with Seamus, Kurt told her, "You were only part of the plan, in that I'd learned the hard way that there's a price for letting someone else raise one's child, or children. It's losing something you can't experience again."

Rory squeezed his arm. "It's okay, Dad," she said, and then she gazed ahead toward Seamus.

His green eyes crinkled in a smile as he watched her approach.

"Does he know?" she said.

"By the end of the course, he'd guessed. He insisted on paying their way. After you agreed to marry him, I couldn't refuse. It would have been rude."

"Mm."

Kurt took his daughter's hand and placed it in Seamus's.

Seamus said, "Thank you."

He and Rory gazed at each other, and a wind rustled paper in the minister's hands, lifting one of the sheets into the wind. He grabbed at it and then had to turn and chase it into the meadow.

"What did you thank him for?" Rory whispered.

"Because of what he told me. That you're the most valuable thing in his life. And he gave you into my keeping."

"Who is giving you into mine?" she asked.

He looked toward the front row, where Belle was crouched down in her dress and white tights, petting Seuss, Lauren was rolling her eyes at something Beau had said and Caleb was folding his program into a paper airline.

Rory and Seamus laughed at the same time.

As the minister made his way back to them with his notes, she said, "Then, I'll have to thank them, too."

* * * * *

REQUEST YOUR FREE BOOKS!
2 FREE WHOLESOME ROMANCE NOVELS IN LARGER PRINT
PLUS 2 FREE MYSTERY GIFTS

꙳꙳꙳꙳꙳꙳꙳꙳꙳꙳꙳꙳꙳꙳꙳꙳꙳꙳꙳

HEARTWARMING™

꙳꙳꙳꙳꙳꙳꙳꙳꙳꙳꙳꙳꙳꙳꙳꙳꙳꙳꙳

Wholesome, tender romances

YES! Please send me 2 FREE Harlequin® Heartwarming Larger Print novels and my 2 FREE mystery gifts (gifts worth about $10). After receiving them, if I don't wish to receive any more books, I can return the shipping statement marked "cancel." If I don't cancel, I will receive 4 brand-new larger-print novels every month and be billed just $4.74 per book in the U.S. or $5.74 per book in Canada. That's a savings of at least 21% off the cover price. It's quite a bargain! Shipping and handling is just 50¢ per book in the U.S. and 75¢ per book in Canada.* I understand that accepting the 2 free books and gifts places me under no obligation to buy anything. I can always return a shipment and cancel at any time. Even if I never buy another book, the two free books and gifts are mine to keep forever.

161/361 IDN FVXV

Name _____ (PLEASE PRINT)

Address _____ Apt. #

City _____ State/Prov. _____ Zip/Postal Code

Signature (if under 18, a parent or guardian must sign)

Mail to the Harlequin® Reader Service:
IN U.S.A.: P.O. Box 1867, Buffalo, NY 14240-1867
IN CANADA: P.O. Box 609, Fort Erie, Ontario L2A 5X3

* Terms and prices subject to change without notice. Prices do not include applicable taxes. Sales tax applicable in N.Y. Canadian residents will be charged applicable taxes. Offer not valid in Quebec. This offer is limited to one order per household. Not valid for current subscribers to Harlequin Hearwarming larger-print books. All orders subject to credit approval. Credit or debit balances in a customer's account(s) may be offset by any other outstanding balance owed by or to the customer. Please allow 4 to 6 weeks for delivery. Offer available while quantities last.

Your Privacy—The Harlequin® Reader Service is committed to protecting your privacy. Our Privacy Policy is available online at www.ReaderService.com or upon request from the Harlequin Reader Service.

We make a portion of our mailing list available to reputable third parties that offer products we believe may interest you. If you prefer that we not exchange your name with third parties, or if you wish to clarify or modify your communication preferences, please visit us at www.ReaderService.com/consumerchoice or write to us at Harlequin Reader Service Preference Service, P.O. Box 9062, Buffalo, NY 14269. Include your complete name and address.

HWDIR13

LARGER-PRINT BOOKS!

GET 2 FREE LARGER-PRINT NOVELS PLUS 2 FREE MYSTERY GIFTS

Love Inspired

Larger-print novels are now available...

LILPDIR13

YES! Please send me the *Cowboy at Heart* collection in Larger Print. This collection begins with 3 FREE books and 2 FREE gifts in the first shipment, and more free gifts will follow! My books will arrive in 8 monthly shipments until I have the entire 51-book *Cowboy at Heart* collection. I will receive 2 or 3 FREE books in each shipment and I will pay just $4.99 U.S./ $5.89 CDN. for each of the other four books in each shipment, plus $2.99 for shipping and handling.* If I decide to keep the entire collection, I'll have paid for only 32 books because 19 books are FREE! I understand that by accepting the 3 free books and gifts places me under no obligation to buy anything. I can always return a shipment and cancel at any time. My free books and gifts are mine to keep no matter what I decide.

256 HCN 0779   456 HCN 0779

Name _____ (PLEASE PRINT) _____

Address _____ Apt. # _____

City _____ State/Prov. _____ Zip/Postal Code _____

Signature (if under 18, a parent or guardian must sign)

Mail to the **Harlequin® Reader Service:**
IN U.S.A.: P.O. Box 1867, Buffalo, NY 14240-1867
IN CANADA: P.O. Box 609, Fort Erie, Ontario L2A 5X3

ReaderService.com

Manage your account online!

- Review your order history
- Manage your payments
- Update your address

*We've designed
the Harlequin® Reader Service
website just for you.*

Enjoy all the features!

- Reader excerpts from any series
- Respond to mailings and special monthly offers
- Discover new series available to you
- Browse the Bonus Bucks catalog
- Share your feedback

Visit us at:
ReaderService.com

RS13

REQUEST YOUR FREE BOOKS!
2 FREE NOVELS PLUS 2 FREE GIFTS!

♦ HARLEQUIN®

SPECIAL EDITION

Life, Love & Family

YES! Please send me 2 FREE Harlequin® Special Edition novels and my 2 FREE gifts (gifts are worth about $10). After receiving them, if I don't wish to receive any more books, I can return the shipping statement marked "cancel." If I don't cancel, I will receive 6 brand-new novels every month and be billed just $4.49 per book in the U.S. or $5.24 per book in Canada. That's a savings of at least 14% off the cover price! It's quite a bargain! Shipping and handling is just 50¢ per book in the U.S. and 75¢ per book in Canada.* I understand that accepting the 2 free books and gifts places me under no obligation to buy anything. I can always return a shipment and cancel at any time. Even if I never buy another book, the two free books and gifts are mine to keep forever.

235/335 HDN FV4K

Name	(PLEASE PRINT)

Address	Apt. #

City	State/Prov.	Zip/Postal Code

Signature (if under 18, a parent or guardian must sign)

Mail to the Harlequin® Reader Service:
IN U.S.A.: P.O. Box 1867, Buffalo, NY 14240-1867
IN CANADA: P.O. Box 609, Fort Erie, Ontario L2A 5X3

Want to try two free books from another line?
Call 1-800-873-8635 or visit www.ReaderService.com.

* Terms and prices subject to change without notice. Prices do not include applicable taxes. Sales tax applicable in N.Y. Canadian residents will be charged applicable taxes. Offer not valid in Quebec. This offer is limited to one order per household. Not valid for current subscribers to Harlequin Special Edition books. All orders subject to credit approval. Credit or debit balances in a customer's account(s) may be offset by any other outstanding balance owed by or to the customer. Please allow 4 to 6 weeks for delivery. Offer available while quantities last.

Your Privacy—The Harlequin® Reader Service is committed to protecting your privacy. Our Privacy Policy is available online at www.ReaderService.com or upon request from the Harlequin Reader Service.

We make a portion of our mailing list available to reputable third parties that offer products we believe may interest you. If you prefer that we not exchange your name with third parties, or if you wish to clarify or modify your communication preferences, please visit us at www.ReaderService.com/consumerschoice or write to us at Harlequin Reader Service Preference Service, P.O. Box 9062, Buffalo, NY 14269. Include your complete name and address.

HSEDIR13

LARGER-PRINT BOOKS!

GET 2 FREE
LARGER-PRINT NOVELS
PLUS 2 FREE
MYSTERY GIFTS

Love Inspired®
SUSPENSE
RIVETING INSPIRATIONAL ROMANCE

Larger-print novels are now available...

REQUEST YOUR FREE BOOKS!
2 FREE NOVELS PLUS 2 FREE GIFTS!

HARLEQUIN®
super romance®

Exciting, emotional, unexpected!

YES! Please send me 2 FREE Harlequin® Superromance® novels and my 2 FREE gifts (gifts are worth about $10). After receiving them, if I don't wish to receive any more books, I can return the shipping statement marked "cancel." If I don't cancel, I will receive 6 brand-new novels every month and be billed just $4.69 per book in the U.S. or $5.24 per book in Canada. That's a savings of at least 15% off the cover price! It's quite a bargain! Shipping and handling is just 50¢ per book in the U.S. and 75¢ per book in Canada.* I understand that accepting the 2 free books and gifts places me under no obligation to buy anything. I can always return a shipment and cancel at any time. Even if I never buy another book, the two free books and gifts are mine to keep forever.

135/336 HDN FV5K

Name	(PLEASE PRINT)	
Address		Apt. #
City	State/Prov.	Zip/Postal Code

Signature (if under 18, a parent or guardian must sign)

Mail to the Harlequin® Reader Service:
IN U.S.A.: P.O. Box 1867, Buffalo, NY 14240-1867
IN CANADA: P.O. Box 609, Fort Erie, Ontario L2A 5X3

**Are you a current subscriber to Harlequin Superromance books
and want to receive the larger-print edition?
Call 1-800-873-8635 or visit www.ReaderService.com.**

* Terms and prices subject to change without notice. Prices do not include applicable taxes. Sales tax applicable in N.Y. Canadian residents will be charged applicable taxes. Offer not valid in Quebec. This offer is limited to one order per household. Not valid for current subscribers to Harlequin Superromance books. All orders subject to credit approval. Credit or debit balances in a customer's account(s) may be offset by any other outstanding balance owed by or to the customer. Please allow 4 to 6 weeks for delivery. Offer available while quantities last.

Your Privacy—The Harlequin® Reader Service is committed to protecting your privacy. Our Privacy Policy is available online at www.ReaderService.com or upon request from the Harlequin Reader Service.

We make a portion of our mailing list available to reputable third parties that offer products we believe may interest you. If you prefer that we not exchange your name with third parties, or if you wish to clarify or modify your communication preferences, please visit us at www.ReaderService.com/consumerschoice or write to us at Harlequin Reader Service Preference Service, P.O. Box 9062, Buffalo, NY 14269. Include your complete name and address.

REQUEST YOUR FREE BOOKS!

2 FREE INSPIRATIONAL NOVELS
PLUS 2
FREE
MYSTERY GIFTS

Love Inspired.
HISTORICAL
INSPIRATIONAL HISTORICAL ROMANCE

YES! Please send me 2 FREE Love Inspired® Historical novels and my 2 FREE mystery gifts (gifts are worth about $10). After receiving them, if I don't wish to receive any more books, I can return the shipping statement marked "cancel." If I don't cancel, I will receive 4 brand-new novels every month and be billed just $4.49 per book in the U.S. or $4.99 per book in Canada. That's a savings of at least 22% off the cover price. It's quite a bargain! Shipping and handling is just 50¢ per book in the U.S. and 75¢ per book in Canada.* I understand that accepting the 2 free books and gifts places me under no obligation to buy anything. I can always return a shipment and cancel at any time. Even if I never buy another book, the two free books and gifts are mine to keep forever.

102/302 IDN FV2V

Name _____ (PLEASE PRINT) _____

Address _____ Apt. # _____

City _____ State/Prov. _____ Zip/Postal Code _____

Signature (if under 18, a parent or guardian must sign) _____

Mail to the Harlequin® Reader Service:
IN U.S.A.: P.O. Box 1867, Buffalo, NY 14240-1867
IN CANADA: P.O. Box 609, Fort Erie, Ontario L2A 5X3

Want to try two free books from another series?
Call 1-800-873-8635 or visit www.ReaderService.com.

* Terms and prices subject to change without notice. Prices do not include applicable taxes. Sales tax applicable in N.Y. Canadian residents will be charged applicable taxes. Offer not valid in Quebec. This offer is limited to one order per household. Not valid for current subscribers to Love Inspired Historical books. All orders subject to credit approval. Credit or debit balances in a customer's account(s) may be offset by any other outstanding balance owed by or to the customer. Please allow 4 to 6 weeks for delivery. Offer available while quantities last.

Your Privacy—The Harlequin® Reader Service is committed to protecting your privacy. Our Privacy Policy is available online at www.ReaderService.com or upon _____ from the Harlequin Reader Service.

_____ a portion of our mailing list available to reputable third parties that offer _____ believe may interest you. If you prefer that we not exchange your name with _____ or If you wish to clarify or modify your communication preferences, please _____ ReaderService.com/consumerschoice or write to us at Harlequin Reader _____ ice Service, P.O. Box 9062, Buffalo, NY 14269. Include your complete _____s.

HSR

LIHDIR13